DANGEROUS LEGACY

Holly is shocked and upset when she learns of the death of her beloved grandfather in America. Then the solicitor tells her the strange conditions of her grandfather's will — she must run his charter boat business in North West Florida for three months before the second part of the legacy is revealed to her. But in Florida danger and adventure lay in wait for Holly — and much more besides . . .

JOYCE JOHNSON

DANGEROUS LEGACY

Complete and Unabridged

LINFORD
Leicester

First published in Great Britain in 1994

First Linford Edition
published 2003

British Library CIP Data

Johnson, Joyce, *1931 –*
    Dangerous legacy.—Large print ed.—
Linford romance library
    1. Love stories
    2. Large type books
    I. Title
    823.9'14 [F]

    ISBN 0–7089–9959–X

Published by
F. A. Thorpe (Publishing)
Anstey, Leicestershire

Set by Words & Graphics Ltd.
Anstey, Leicestershire
Printed and bound in Great Britain by
T. J. International Ltd., Padstow, Cornwall

This book is printed on acid-free paper

1

Holly turned the heater control to maximum and recoiled as an icy blast hit her in the face. Grandad's truck was of the vintage variety and its air-conditioning system had a mind of its own! She pulled the lever back and now hot air streamed through the vents. She shrugged philosophically — the waterfront couldn't be far away and it would probably be slightly cooler by the ocean.

The early September heat in Florida could be fierce. She'd expected that, but hadn't been prepared for the stifling humidity.

The steering-wheel of Fred Peters' pick-up was sticky with heat and grease — that was to be expected, too. Her grandad had never seen the point of spending time on what he considered the 'non necessities' of life, like house or vehicle cleaning.

'Time enough for that when I'm old,' he'd said so many times, as he'd whisked her off from her boarding-school on the last day of term on one of their adventure trips.

Holly remembered the stares of her school-mates, as Fred Peters had swept up the gravelled drive, either towing a large, ancient caravan, or a disreputable looking bargain of a second-hand motor home. Over the years, those stares had turned to envy, as Fred's eccentricity and charm had won the admiration of her peers, and it became a regular event, guessing which exotic place Holly and Fred were off to next.

She never told anyone that it was part of the bargain struck with her grandfather — she'd stay at the hated boarding-school without running away, just so long as Fred rescued her in the holidays, and took her miles away from the rigid rules and regulations of term time.

They had both kept to that bargain

and their travels together throughout both Western and Eastern Europe had forged a bond as strong as tempered steel between them. They'd never made it to America together. Although Holly had longed to visit the States, Fred had been curiously reluctant.

'One day maybe, when you're older. Time enough, plenty of other places to see first,' he told the young Holly, who depended on him so much as her only remaining family.

She'd gone along with him, of course, but even then she sensed there was something else behind his decision, other than a general reluctance for her to cross the Atlantic.

'Now I'll never know why. I should have come over sooner, to take care of you, but you always were stubborn — and independent.' Holly pulled up at a red light intersection, and brushed away a tear. Three months since he'd died, and here she was, still talking to him!

Three months — three years — thirty

years? The grief would lessen, but the gap he left in her young life would never be filled, she knew that. The wonderful, flamboyant character who'd been her grandfather for twenty-three years would always have a special place in her heart. That was why she was now in North West Florida, driving to a fishing resort on the Gulf of Mexico on this sticky day in early September. She knew exactly where she was going. Grandfather's instructions were precise on that point — if inconclusive on the rest of it!

Two weeks earlier, a phone call had turned Holly's world upside down. James Spencer, junior partner of London solicitors, Chapman and Spencer, had informed her politely that her grandfather was dead.

The dry, bald statement failed to penetrate, and it was impossible to concentrate, her mind drifting away, as she heard snatches of information.

'So sorry about the delay . . . identification on the body doubtful . . . Mr

Peter's lawyer in Florida has instructed us to . . . ' and incredibly, ' . . . dead for some time, his boat drifting in the Gulf of Mexico.' Then after a long pause, 'Could you come to the office as soon as possible?'

'What for?' Holly heard her own voice, strangely hoarse.

She didn't register the puzzled note in the lawyer's voice. 'It's customary. There's a will. Your grandfather's will is, to say the least, not of the usual pattern.'

'All right. I'll . . . I'll ring you tomorrow.'

'Why not make an appointment now?'

But Holly had put the phone down as the tears began to flow. It was two days before she felt composed enough to ring the lawyers again.

James Spencer looked relieved that she'd turned up at the office as arranged! He paid hasty condolences, then took out a large envelope.

'It's all very unusual, Miss Peters.

We've acted for your grandfather over the years on various matters, but he made this latest will in Florida. His U.S. solicitor, Homer Rechts, has, in accordance with his client's specific instructions, sent us just the first part. Your grandfather — er — appears to have bequeathed you a bit of a puzzle. Perhaps I could go through the terms of the will with you. There's a letter, too, marked 'Confidential — for Holly.' The will first, perhaps?'

Holly nodded. It was harder than she'd imagined to keep calm — even harder to associate her very lively grandfather with a will, and all that that entailed.

'First, Mr Spencer, I have to know — how did my grandfather die? You said on the phone something about being in a boat.'

Again he coughed nervously and avoided her direct look. 'The judge ruled 'Death by misadventure.' It was hard to identify the body, it had been in the water for so long. An autopsy showed a heart attack, but I doubt if we shall ever know the exact circumstances. I'm so sorry, Miss — Holly.'

'But not even to be at the funeral! Why wasn't I told earlier?'

James Spencer shrugged his shoulders expressively. 'Unfortunately, the boat, which was found some days later, was registered in Mexico. The authorities there took charge, and they're not bound by United States' law. They probably wanted to clear up the case quickly.'

As Holly put her hand to her eyes, James looked alarmed, and made a move towards her.

'I'm all right, really.' She looked up at him brightly and with an effort, said, 'You can tell me about the will now.'

'It's quite simple, although rather different from the norm. In my experience, I don't think I've come across a two-part legacy before.' James was relieved to be dealing with practicalities.

'Legacy? I didn't think Grandad had

anything to leave.'

'He wasn't a rich man.' The solicitor scanned the paper in front of him. 'But your grandfather has left you a charter-boat business in North West Florida.'

'What?' Holly's eyes widened.

James Spencer hurried on. 'It's called 'Jade Bay Charters' — on the Emerald Coast.'

'But, Grandad — he's never owned a boat in his life — never shown the least interest . . . '

'Nevertheless, that's what he's left you. Plus a sum of money — sufficient to live on for, perhaps, a year. Plus the lease on an apartment at . . . ' He consulted the paper again. ' . . . Silver Shores, San Maria, North West Florida.'

Holly shook her head in bewilderment. 'But what am I do to with a charter-boat business?'

'Ah, now that's the really strange part! You have to assume ownership as a working employer, and run it for a

8

minimum period of three months. You have to prove to Mr Peters' Florida lawyer that you've successfully done that and then, if they're satisfied, they'll release part two of Mr Peters' will. On the other hand,' he continued, as his client appeared totally dumbfounded, 'you are at liberty to sell it, from here in the United Kingdom, or after you've seen it, from Florida. But if you do that, the second part of the will is to be destroyed without you seeing it. I told you, it's an unusual case.'

After a pause, Holly spoke. 'I don't know what to say. Grandad is — was an unusual man, but this . . . '

James Spencer stood up. 'Why don't you take a look at the letter he's written? It may explain his motives a little.' He passed an envelope to her. 'There's a copy of the apartment lease, a vehicle log book and maps.'

'Please, if it's all right, I'd like to look at it on my own for a few moments.'

James Spencer smiled. 'Of course. I'll

arrange coffee for us.' Holly gave him a grateful smile.

As he left the room, Holly drew out the documents and began to read. It was a tactful ten minutes later before James Spencer returned with a tray of coffee and a plate of his secretary's favourite chocolate biscuits. Holly was standing with her back to the door, staring unseeingly over the city. She turned and James Spender saw her soft, brown eyes were moist with unshed tears. She was controlling her emotions with difficulty. Forgetting the proprieties, he put the tray on his desk, crossed to where she was standing, and put his arm around her shoulder.

'I'm so sorry. It has all been a great shock to you — Mr Peters' sudden death, and now this.' He gestured towards the envelope and led her back to the chair. 'You've read everything?'

'Yes,' Holly replied shakily. 'I'm all right. Just a bit . . . stunned, and surprised, though I shouldn't be surprised at anything Grandad does — did!'

'Sit down. Have your coffee.' Mr Spender fussed around her, offering milk, sugar and biscuits.

Holly blew her nose. She was grateful for his concern.

'Thanks. I feel better. You know, for the first time since I heard he was . . . dead, I believe it, and yet I feel he's with me, too. That doesn't make sense, does it?'

James stirred his coffee and thought awhile. 'In the circumstances, I think it does. Perhaps that was his intention. If you do as he requests, you will be sort of together for a while.'

He steepled his fingers in a prayer position on his desk.

'What your grandfather wants you to do is . . . ' He chose his words with care, not wanting to upset her. 'It's a little odd, and would mean consider-able rearrangement of your life for a while. You have a job, and — forgive me, I don't mean to pry — a boyfriend?' Such an attractive, and he guessed, normally vivacious girl, must

11

have a fiancé, or partner, at least! 'I believe, the last time I saw Mr Peters, you were just finishing college. Marine Biology, if I recall?'

Holly nodded ruefully. 'That's right, but I haven't got a permanent job yet. I've just had a series of temps. The job's not a problem.'

Dave was another matter, she thought. If she decided to go to the States, would he want to go with her? Did she want him to? Or was this something between herself and her grandfather which she should tackle alone?

James Spencer gave her a shrewd look. 'I should remind you, you don't actually need to disrupt your life at all. Have you considered the other option? You can carry on with your life here and leave us, and your American lawyers, to sell the business your grandfather left you.'

'But if I don't take it on, I don't get to see the second part of the will, isn't that it?'

He nodded confirmation. 'That's correct. I've no idea what the business is worth, or what state it's in.'

'Not very flourishing, according to Grandad's letter.'

'Perhaps all the more reason for selling?'

'Take the money and run?' Holly interrupted, lifting her head. 'No thanks. You've been very kind, Mr Spencer, but I've really no choice. Grandad's spirit would never let me rest if I turned this down. I've got to carry it through. You met him, didn't you? So you know that he was not a man made in the common mould.' She held out her hand. 'I must go to Florida — at least to take a look at his legacy.'

'Shall I contact Jade Bay Charters? I can let whoever is in charge know you're coming.'

Holly considered for a moment. 'I don't think so. I think I'd rather just arrive and see how things are when I get there. I'll be in touch.'

That interview seemed a long time

ago, but in fact it had taken Holly only a couple of weeks to tie up her job, rent out her flat — and deal with Dave. The latter had been unexpectedly easy. Although they had been going out for six months, both had avoided discussion on any long-term commitment. Dave was a workaholic, the financial markets taking up most of his time, and when Holly told him about the will, his reaction was predictable.

'I'll miss you like crazy, Holly, but I couldn't leave here now. Things here are much too volatile, and this idea of your grandfather's is totally ridiculous. He doesn't even say what the second part of the deal would be — just an adventure which could make you a fortune. I'd get rid of the business he's left you, if I were you. Charter boats, isn't it? It's bound to be a white elephant. Invest the proceeds.'

Holly laughed. 'With you, I suppose.'

'You could do worse,' he had said, good-naturedly.

With a firm shake of her head, Holly

tried to clear the past and concentrate on the present. The present and the future were what mattered — and fulfilling Grandfather's last will and testament. Concentrating on the road, she looked for signs. The highway directions were clear. 'Beaches straight on, Waterfront Marina to the right'. She swung the heavy pick-up off the main highway and followed the right-hand turn.

She parked the truck at the top of an incline leading to the dock, which was packed with vessels of all shapes and sizes. All along the waterfront, bill-boards advertised charter trips into the Gulf; deep-sea fishing, scuba diving and snorkelling. On the board-walk, boat crews were gutting, cleaning and bagging fish which the tourists had caught.

A breeze stirred the masts to a tinny clanking as she started to walk towards the boats. She couldn't suppress a sudden shiver of nervousness. It had all seemed straightforward enough in

London and the trip, so far, had been fun. It felt like a holiday, and she was enjoying being in America. The reality she'd have to face now was a bit more daunting.

There were many more charter companies than she'd expected. All the names sounded familiar, and she wished she'd looked at the documents again last night. She'd meant to, but there'd been so much to do, settling into the apartment, getting used to the truck . . .

The heat beaded her upper lip with sweat, and from her shorts' pocket, she took out a scrunch band, lifted her heavy hair from her neck, and pushed it into a pony tail. That felt cooler, and it was then she saw the green and black lettering on one of the boats, JADE BAY CHARTERS. This must be it! Holly's stomach knotted, her eyes misted and she stepped blindly across the gang plank on to the deck of the nearest boat with the name.

'What d'ya want, girl?'

Startled, Holly looked up, squinting in the strong sunlight. The woman standing way above her on the high deck was tall, with a mass of tight, springing blonde curls. Her voice was harsh.

'We've no jobs. We don't take casuals.'

'I'm not . . . '

'Too many of you youngsters want a few hours here and there, then clear off. Move along now.' The woman leaned over and pointed off the deck.

Holly frowned. She knew that in shorts and sneakers, hair pulled back and skin bare of make-up, she could perhaps be mistaken for a college student, but the woman's tone was more hostile than any she'd encountered during her brief stay in the States.

Moving forward to stand directly beneath the blonde, Holly spoke sharply.

'Excuse me; I don't want a job. I'm not a student. I've come to . . . '

But already the girl had moved

17

swiftly down the ladder to the bottom deck.

'OK, OK, sorry. If it's scuba or snorkelling, there's a party starting out from the Eastern jetty in ten minutes. Mike Klonska's boat — over there.'

Holly's voice rose in exasperation.

'Nor have I come to dive — yet. I've come from London to . . . '

A man's voice sliced through her protest. 'What's the problem, Crystal?'

Holly tilted her head. The voice came from above, and where the blonde had previously stood, a broad figure now blocked the sunlight. His outline, against the sun, was dark. To Holly's fanciful imagination, he appeared to tower over the two women below like a sea giant! But he looked at Holly with very human curiosity.

'Hi, who are you?' he asked but Crystal cut in.

'She's just another kid hanging around. I've told her, Mike's setting out on a scuba party . . . '

'Hold on. A customer's a customer.

No call to go shipping her off to the opposition.'

He leaned comfortably over the rail, eying Holly in a leisurely fashion. Crystal's disparaging stare made it clear what she thought of Holly's paying potential.

'Jedd, she's just a kid. We haven't got time. The Texans'll be along in a minute.'

'There's no need to be rude,' he rebuked, 'and the Texans are usually a mite late. Also, I believe you underestimate the young lady.' The voice was warm, richly melodic, with a slight trace of the Southern drawl to which Holly had become acclimatised during the past few days. He spoke again, and her heart skipped as she felt the intensity of his dark-eyed scrutiny.

'I'm Jedd Rivers and this is Crystal Bankston, my partner. What can we do for you?'

The smile was friendly and encouraging, but Holly was dry-mouthed. Had she made a mistake? She must be on the wrong boat. Either this wasn't Jade Bay Charter Company, or she'd got the name wrong. Either way, it didn't fit her grandfather's description of a run-down operation. This powerful, confident-looking man was in obvious control. The boat was a sleek fifty-footer with modern radar and electronic sonic equipment. Alongside was a larger, rigged schooner, also under the Jade Bay logo, and about to embark with a full complement of tourists aboard.

Jedd was still smiling. Crystal's scowl had deepened. Both of them were waiting for her to reply. Desperately, she looked around. She needed to play for time. She noticed the fishing rods neatly stacked on deck.

'I'd like to — try the fishing.'

It sounded unlikely, and Holly didn't miss the sharp glance Crystal exchanged with Jedd as she snapped, 'We're all booked.'

'No.' Jedd leaned out over the rail. 'We had a cancellation, remember? In any case, Miss — er — won't take up a

20

great deal of space.' He ran his eyes over Holly's small, shapely figure. 'I'm coming down. It's kinda tiring carrying on a conversation by distance.'

In a second, Jedd was with them, on the same ground level, but still looking down at Holly. He held out his hand.

'Hi again — English, I guess. London, you said? Back-packing?'

'No.'

At close quarters, she saw that Jedd Rivers was a craggy, attractive man in his late twenties, possibly thirty. Tipping back her head to look at him, she saw the faintest of laughter lines round his dark eyes, a wide generous mouth, strong, even, white teeth. An easy smile reflected a general air of lazy, beguiling grace which was sensually appealing. Holly found it hard to look away. He finally let go of her hand, his expression still enquiring.

She repeated, 'No, not back-packing. I'm here on business.'

His eyes widened. 'Business? In the Gulf? What would that be?'

It could be very much his business, but she was beginning to doubt it. Even so, she saw little point in explaining just yet.

'Oh, just some odds and ends,' she said vaguely. 'Now, may I take a rod?'

He laughed and touched her shoulder lightly. 'Why sure, if that's what you want. Crystal'll fix you up. And — here's the rest of the party. Let me get them settled. I didn't catch your name.'

'Holly Peters.'

Her voice was lost in the laughter and greetings of a noisy group heading for the boat. Jedd went out to meet them, but the look he threw at Holly was speculative. He'd automatically registered her shapely figure and clear brown-eyed stare. She did look such a kid, but there was also a steely quality, and calm maturity of purpose about her which told her that Crystal had misjudged the English girl. Holly, whatever her name was, was no college kid.

The next few hours were bliss for Holly, and she nearly forgot why she'd come to Florida. Sea Jade 1 had been chartered by a group of fishermen and their wives, from Texas. They were all so taken with Holly, her accent and her inexperience with a rod, that they took her under their collective wing to show her how to fish, and turned the whole expedition into a party.

It was fun! The breeze was cool, the water a clear, translucent green. She could see why this part of Florida was named the Emerald Coast — and away on shore, the white beaches fringed the dunes like bleached sandpaper. Holly soaked up the hot sun and balmy sea air, hoping that this was how her grandfather had spent his last months. He would have loved it, she knew that.

She caught a couple of red snapper fish which a crewman promised to gut and clean for her supper. Then she stowed her rod and line to watch the pleasure of the more serious fishermen.

After a couple of hours, Sea Jade

turned to head back to harbour. Jedd handed over the wheel to Crystal and came to stand beside Holly.

'You didn't fish for long.'

'No, but I've caught enough for my supper. I'm enjoying watching the others.'

'You're staying locally?'

'Yes.'

'Nearby? Are you with friends?' Jedd's questions were casual, but Holly sensed a purpose behind them which was more than just friendly curiosity.

'You ask a lot of questions, Mr Rivers.' She moved away — he was too close for comfort. His bare forearm, brushing hers, had sent a tremor of alarm through her.

He persisted. 'Are you in town, or on the beach?'

'I've an apartment on the beach.'

'It's a big beach. Where exactly?'

'Look, we're nearly back. Shouldn't you help Crystal dock or something?'

'Crystal's very capable of docking the entire fleet single-handed. She doesn't need my help. It's you I'm interested in. I think you're here at Emerald Bay for a purpose — other than fishing — and at the Jade Bay Charter Company particularly.'

The waterfront was only yards away, the docking berth close. Crystal confidently nudged the vessel to a halt. The Texan fishermen packed up picnic boxes, joking, comparing catches.

'You did OK, Holly.' A huge Texan clapped her on the shoulder. 'Great fishing, Jedd. We'll be booking a night session with Jade Bay again soon. You're the best round here. Maybe see you again, Holly?'

'Maybe.' She smiled.

She must have got it wrong. This company, run so efficiently by Jedd and Crystal, couldn't be that described in her grandfather's letter. As Crystal slid the boat snugly into its berth, Holly looked up at the wheel-deck, admiring the girl's skill. They'd come into the berth alongside the one they'd left, and were now facing a different way. There

25

was no mistake — the board swinging above the berth shouted the facts: JADE BAY CHARTERS. Proprietor FRED PETERS.

Holly felt a wave of emotion. It was her grandfather's business — hers now. She felt his steadying influence near her. He'd probably been on this very boat dozens of times.

Crystal was already out on the board-walk, the boat tied securely. The Texans were booking their next trip, and Jedd and Holly were the only ones left on board. She turned to face him.

'You're right,' she said. 'I'm sorry, I misled you a little. I am here on business, and it does concern you. I'm Holly Peters, Fred Peter's granddaughter, and I've come to take over JADE BAY CHARTERS.'

2

Jedd Rivers didn't seem at all surprised. Pushing back the baseball cap which, to Holly, seemed obligatory for all American men, he continued to look down at her, waiting for her to continue. Holly was forced to break the silence.

'I'm sorry, but I'm here to run Jade Bay Charters.'

'If you have to, you have to, though you'll be a little different from the usual run of bosses around here.' Jedd's reply was laconic. 'It's no big deal for me, and it's no more than I expected all along. I knew you were here for more than just a couple of red snappers!'

'But — won't you mind?' Holly was surprised at Jedd's ready acceptance of her presence.

'Mind? Why should I? I've done what I came to do. This is a going concern now. I don't know what your qualifications are, Miss Holly Peters, but I doubt you've much experience of this type of deep-sea fishing. Crystal and I have done a good rescue job here. She's local, born and bred — part of the fishing community. That's helped a lot.' His eyes narrowed. 'You're going to start hiring from scratch?'

Holly bit her lip, feeling foolish, wishing she hadn't blurted out her news so impulsively. She hadn't give much thought to the actual running of the business. She'd imagined, from her grandfather's letter, that it was a much smaller concern — maybe just a single charter boat and certainly not dominated by two such powerful personalities as Jedd and Crystal.

A year earlier, she'd seen her grandfather off at Heathrow Airport, bound for the West Coast of the United States. Fred Peters reckoned his job of bringing up his granddaughter was more or less done when she'd finished college and found a job. 'You're on your own for a bit, Holly. I'm off for a spell, to see what the States has to offer. I'll be in touch.'

Their farewell had been emotional, but Holly had never expected it to be final. He'd sent postcards from every state, working eastwards across the continent. His final card had hinted of great news to come, after a trip to Atlanta, and a 'spot of re-organisation.' He'd ended the card, 'I'll soon be ready for you over here'. After that, there was silence for weeks . . . until the dreadful day in James Spencer's office.

'Holly?' The questioning voice cut across her thoughts. 'Are you listening? What's the matter?'

She pulled herself together with an effort. 'Nothing — I just hadn't expected to find Jade Bay in such a flourishing state.'

'It wasn't, until fairly recently. Crystal will have to be told why you've come. You must tell her, too.'

'Of course I will. I — I just wanted to make sure I'd come to the right place. Until I saw Grandad's name on the board . . . you see, he didn't describe Jade Bay like this.' She indicated the swish lines of the boat, the adjacent schooner, the general air of affluence.

'Fred Peters — your grandfather, eh?'

'How well did you know him?'

'I don't think we should say any more without Crystal being here. She's my partner and she should know about your plans for her future. I'll go fetch her. Maybe you could make us all coffee. The galley's below.' He pointed down the stairway, then strode off along the board-walk. There was no sign of Crystal, but Jedd obviously knew where to find her.

For the first time since arriving in America, Holly felt isolated and uncertain, the adrenalin of the challenge of her grandfather's mysterious adventure draining away. Dave's advice came back to her — put the whole outfit on the market, and forget about it. Now she'd met Jedd Rivers and Crystal Bankston, they'd surely be keen buyers. And yet, even as the thought trickled into her mind, she dismissed it as cowardly weakness. She had to know what was in the second part of the will. She smiled ruefully — Grandad certainly knew how to appeal to her sense of adventure — even from beyond the grave.

She went to make the coffee. The machine was all set, and all it needed was switching on. Putting three mugs on a tray, she looked around for milk and sugar to carry up on deck, then voices above made her hesitate. One was strident, the other calmly reasonable. Before she could climb the stairway, a blonde fury hurled herself down. Jedd followed more slowly, but was close enough to put a restraining hand on Crystal's shoulder.

'Don't fly off the handle. You haven't heard yet . . . '

'I know what she's come for! I knew as soon as I saw her — and when I heard that accent. I knew it had to be . . . '

'All I said was Fred Peters' granddaughter's finally arrived.'

31

Jedd's placatory tone seemed to fuel Crystal's fury all the more.

'She's come to take Jade Bay, hasn't she?' She strode up close to Holly, who backed away in alarm at the anger sparkling from the girl's grey eyes. 'Haven't you?' Crystal directly accused, shaking off Jedd's hand.

'Just a minute. Holly's made coffee. Let's take it on deck and discuss this in a civilised way. I'm sure there's no intention . . . '

'Civilised! Intention! It's all right for you, Jedd. It doesn't mean so much to you, even though you've worked like a dog. Both of us have, and Brett — and now look what's happened. He should have left it to us — he promised! But then, Fred Peters was just a crazy old fool!'

This time it was Holly who drew herself up tall, anger boiling.

'Don't you dare speak about my grandfather like that. What right have you?'

'I've every right,' Crystal yelled at

her, almost spitting in temper. 'He left us to run this place. It was a dump! And until Jedd turned up, it paid peanuts. We worked for nothing, but he was always promising we'd be rich. It should be our business. He was never here. We had to do everything, while he went off with that other mad fool. A pair of old lunatics!'

'Crystal!' Jedd's voice whiplashed across the small space. 'That's enough. Just cool off. Let's hear Holly's plans. It's been a shock, but you knew Fred had a granddaughter. What did you expect?'

'Oh, yes, we knew. He talked enough about her. But we didn't expect the old fool to die and . . . '

'Stop it! You're getting hysterical. The man's dead, and his granddaughter's raw in grief still. Have some pity, for goodness' sake.'

Holly blinked. 'Perhaps I should leave,' she said hurriedly. 'We'll talk later.' She handed a card to Crystal. 'Here's my address and phone number.

I'm truly sorry it was such a shock, my turning up like this, but it's been a shock for me, too, coming here, seeing his name like that. I only learned of his death two weeks ago.'

Crystal glanced at the card but didn't take it. 'No — I'm going. But I'm not putting up with it — you'll see.' With a baleful glare at Holly, she stormed out.

Legs shaking, Holly sat down on a stool. 'I haven't said anything yet. Why is she so cross?'

'Oh, don't let Crystal get to you. She's a volatile kinda girl, but it's been tough for her these last few months. She shouldn't have spoken about your grandpa like that,' Jedd said, a touch apologetically.

'No, she shouldn't. He wasn't crazy, and he was certainly no fool.'

'You were fond of him, weren't you?' he said gently.

'Of course I was. I loved him. Since Grandma died, he was all I had.' Holly couldn't prevent the slight catch in her voice.

'No parents — other family?'

'My parents were killed when I was eleven. Grandma and Grandad brought me up.' She clenched her fists tightly and forced herself to think of other things. 'But I'm sure you don't want to hear the story of my life, Mr Rivers. I can see it was clumsy of me, letting Crystal find out in such an abrupt way. I'll be back tomorrow, or the next day, if you think that's not too soon. Perhaps I could meet the others then — I presume there are more?'

'We had to take on more staff recently, but they're mainly part-time casuals. The regulars are Crystal, Captain Andy and myself. Apart from Crystal and Andy, the others won't care who runs the show, just so long as they're paid regularly. We're pretty well booked through tomorrow. End of the day would be best, when we're all free. About seven o'clock, when the fishing's done?'

'It's a long day!'

'First boat's out at seven — sometimes five or six. No point wasting the day. Work hard — play hard. The season doesn't last all year round, so we have to make it while we can. So, would half-past-seven tomorrow evening be OK?'

'Fine,' Holly said vaguely, her eyes drawn to Jedd's very dark, blue eyes. On deck, in the sunlight, they'd been a startling clear sapphire in his tanned, out-of-doors face. Yet his hands were well-cared-for city hands.

'Holly — did you hear me?'

She jumped. 'No. Sorry, I was — er — thinking about the meeting.'

'Don't worry about it. I asked if you'd like to eat — have a bite of supper with me tonight? Maybe we could talk over your plans and get to know each other a bit — and I don't mind hearing the story of your life.'

'I'm not sure.'

Holly was confused. The whole situation had thrown her off balance. She'd been hoping to get used to the area and settle in slowly but she found herself in a state of mild shock. Jade

Bay wasn't a bit as she'd expected. And Jedd Rivers was a complete surprise!

'What about Crystal?' she asked. 'I thing you said that she should be present at any talk about the future.'

'Leave Crystal to me.' Jedd's reply was easy, confident. 'It'll maybe take a while for her to come off the boil. You needn't say anything about the business tonight if you don't want to, and she'll be OK by tomorrow evening.'

Such positive conviction must come from close, personal knowledge. Holly had noticed how protective Jedd was towards his partner, and wondered how deep the relationship was. Jedd picked up her card, which Crystal had refused.

'Silver Shores Apartments. You really are right on the beach there. I'll call for you around six. I'll get some of the paperwork up to date and bring it with me, ready for you to study tomorrow. If you'll excuse me now, I'll make a start.'

The dismissal was firmly authorative. Holly felt like the employee, not the employer! His next question high-lighted it even more.

'By the way, do you have any experience in this type of operation?'

'I've a college degree in business studies.'

He looked unimpressed. 'I mean practical experience. You obviously know nothing about fishing, and that's what most of our clients come for. There are snorkelling trips, too, and scuba diving. Have you done any of that?'

'Are you interviewing me?' Holly tried to look stern and dignified.

'No. I just don't want the company to slide downhill — again.'

'It won't. I'll see you tomorrow. We'll talk about it then, Mr Rivers.'

'Jedd, please. You've forgotten already that we're having dinner tonight? Such a memory can't be good for business. See you later, Holly.' His smile was mocking as he scooped up a pile of log sheets and folders and left the cabin.

He seemed pretty sure that I

wouldn't refuse, Holly thought, as she heard his footsteps across the deck above. She waited a few minutes before following, congratulating herself that she'd evaded some of his questions. She might need a few trump cards at tomorrow's meeting. An ace or two might be the only way to steal an advantage over the confident Jedd Rivers.

Ten minutes later, she was back in the truck. It was still very hot, and walking up the incline had made her sticky. She thought longingly of the air-conditioned apartment and a cool shower — maybe even a swim in the ocean first. But the day had been ill-omened right from the start and her troubles weren't over yet. The truck refused to start. The old engine gurgled once, spluttered and died.

The truck and apartment were part of Fred's legacy. He'd taken the apartment on a two-year lease six months earlier, when he'd first arrived in Florida, although, according to the janitor who'd given her the keys, he'd spent very little time there. Just as Crystal had said earlier!

The apartment was in a block, purpose-built for vacation rental. Holly loved its modern amenities, and wonderful Gulf view from the wooden deck, spanning two sides. The truck was another matter. It was old, temperamental and a terrible gas-guzzler, and she knew that the sensible thing would be to ditch it and buy a car. But that seemed disloyal to her grandfather.

The vehicle had something of his eccentric spirit. He must have driven it along the inter-coastal highways, and there were a couple of American-style caps in the back — she could just imagine him wearing those! Holly felt so close to him when she was in the truck, she knew it would be hard to part with it. Unfortunately, she wasn't much of a mechanic!

Getting out, she wondered where the nearest garage was. There was one back by the apartment, but she hadn't noticed one on the way down. Before she could start back to the waterfront to ask, a car drew alongside, and a dark-haired, olive-skinned man wound down his window.

'Anything wrong? Need any help here?'

He was middle-aged, and the woman by his side had similar colouring. Mexican or Hispanic, Holly guessed.

'I'm afraid my truck won't start. Is there a garage nearby?'

'Might be just a little thing. Want me to try it?'

'Well . . . ' Holly hesitated. The woman looked none too pleased, perhaps resenting her husband's gallantry to a young girl, but the man was already out of his car. 'Are you sure it's not too much trouble? Have you got the time?'

'Sure do. All the time in the world. We're on vacation.' He held out his hand. 'Jamez Ramirez and Anna, my wife. From Mexico.'

'Holly Peters — London.'

'Guessed you were English.' His wife got out of the car and she also shook hands, but Holly noted her dark eyes narrowed, and the smile never reached beyond her mouth.

'I can walk to a garage,' Holly started, but Jamez had already tried the motor, and was lifting the bonnet.

'I tell you — it's no problem. Simple, you've overheated. Bone dry. It's possible the cylinder's cracked. You'll surely need a garage. Hop in — we'll take you. There's one back along, about a mile.'

'I couldn't possibly . . . ' Holly stammered but the woman had already opened the passenger door and her smile was warmer.

'Please. It won't take long — and — we're thinking of a trip to Britain next year. Maybe you could give us a few tips.'

As Holly went to get into the car, grateful for the lift, she happened to glance back towards the dock and caught sight of Crystal in a phone booth near the top of the incline. It was nearly a hundred yards away, but Holly could see the anger expressed in the girl's body, one hand clamping the receiver to her ear, the other repeatedly pushing though her hair, dragging it into spiky tangles.

As she turned in agitation, Holly saw her face was flushed and tear-stained. Then she noticed Holly, and her start of surprise turned instantly to a grimace of bitter dislike. Slamming down the receiver, she ran from the phone box, back towards the boats.

Instinctively, Holly turned to follow. She couldn't bear the thought that she'd caused such distress, and felt she must have it out with Crystal. But Anna Ramirez was ushering her into the car, and the moment was lost.

They drove her to a garage, and waited. All the mechanics were busy — it would take a while to send someone to pick up the truck. It was already four o'clock, and it would probably be the morning before they could help. Holly shrugged. There was nothing she could do about it. She reported back to the Ramirez.

'Thanks, you've been so kind . . . '

'How're you getting home?' Anna asked.

'Taxi. Hitch. Bus!'

'Nonsense. We'll take you. Where do you live?'

'Silver Shores, on Henderson Beach.'

'That's not far from where we're staying. It's unlikely you'll find a bus, and it wouldn't be safe for a young girl like you to hitch.'

'I'll be OK.' Holly protested. 'This part of Florida is as safe as houses.'

'No, no, we insist.' Jamez backed up his wife. 'Come on, won't take long.'

Holly had been charmed by the good-natured friendliness of all the Americans, and now Mexicans, she'd met so far. Crystal Bankston was the only exception. She smiled warmly at her rescuers.

'Well, thanks, but in return, I insist you stay for a cup of tea!'

'It's a deal.' Jamez smiled broadly. 'It would be criminal not to take the opportunity of sampling a real British cup of tea!'

They left the garage, and headed back through the main street of the resort, turning off along the road to the beaches. Holly sat back to enjoy the ride, but couldn't forget the look of dark malice she'd seen on Crystal's face, and wondered again what she'd done to cause such instant aversion. There was obviously a lot that she didn't know about the history of Jade Bay Charters.

Well, she thought, I'll soon find out. Crystal will see to that, I'm sure.

3

By the time the Ramirez had had tea, admired the view and taken her phone number with a promise to meet up again real soon, Holly had only quarter of an hour to shower and change. When Jedd rang through the security intercom system at the front door, her hair was still damp from the shower, hanging round her shoulders in thick, satin swatches.

She knew it would soon dry off in the warm air, and as she didn't want to ask Jedd into the apartment, she picked up her bag to meet him at the door — and caught her breath! His tall frame filled the doorway; dark-blue, silk shirt and expensive-looking darker trousers moulded his body, adding elegant sophistication to the casual, easy grace.

Holly looked doubtfully at her informal, low-cut sundress.

'I didn't think to dress up. You said a bit of supper!'

'I'm not dressed up,' he said with a genuine smile. 'It's just a change from fisherman's gear. Anything goes here, and you look lovely.' He took her jacket and placed it round her shoulders, his fingers brushing her bare skin. 'The car's open-topped. You might feel chilly and your hair's damp.'

Holly began to feel strangely light-headed — from hunger probably, she told herself. As she stepped out of the door, she was in for another surprise. Jedd's sports car was a long, silver streak that shrieked money. She looked at him suspiciously. Everything about Jedd Rivers denied the fact he was an employed boatman. He had all the trappings of wealth, and it was impossible to believe that it came from the profits, or his salary, from Jade Bay Charters.

He helped her into the passenger seat with exquisite courtesy, before sliding in beside her.

'Warm enough? Do you want the top up?'

'I'm all right, thanks. Don't forget, I'm English. This is a heatwave compared to the climate we have. I'm used to the cold.'

'Maybe that's where you get your national reputation from?'

'What's that?'

'Reserved ice-maidens,' he said gravely.

'I'm — we're not! That's a ridiculous myth.'

'I didn't say you, Holly. I couldn't, for one moment, believe that you're made of ice.' He turned to look at her, blue eyes innocently wide, eyebrows raised only slightly.

She flushed. 'I wish you wouldn't treat me like a schoolgirl.'

Jedd swung the car into a parking lot overlooking the beach. 'Wouldn't dream of it. After all, you're the boss — from tomorrow.'

She bit her lip. He was still teasing her.

★ ★ ★

During the meal, Jedd chatted about the United States in general, and Florida in particular, keeping the conversation strictly neutral, avoiding any mention of Jade Bay or Fred Peters.

The Pelican Restaurant was one of the smartest Holly had been in. Normally, she would have revelled in its elegant atmosphere, especially combined with the attention of such an attractive man as the American opposite her. But her stomach churned rebelliously as she tried to keep her composure in his charming company.

'How about coffee, Holly? We can have it here, or shall we move on?'

'I'd love coffee — here.' Pull yourself together, she admonished herself sharply. He'll be walking all over you at tomorrow's meeting! She sat up straight. 'This is a lovely place. Thanks for bringing me here.'

'My pleasure.'

The waiter arrived, and Holly looked at Jedd from under her thick lashes as she sipped the delicious, aromatic coffee he had poured. Then he tilted back in his chair and smiled.

'So, Holly Peters, you've come to take us over. Do you want to talk about it? It seems to be more of a surprise to you than it does to me.'

She made up her mind. It would be good to confide in someone, and although he tended to treat her like a backward child, Jedd Rivers was a man of strength, whom she instinctively felt she could trust. Oddly, she felt her grandfather's approval of that decision. She shivered.

'Are you cold?' Jedd asked solicitously. 'Maybe we should go.'

'No — please. I like it here, with all the lights around the bay — it's pretty.'

Jedd poured more coffee for both of them, and waited. Holly gave a small cough, and twisted her long hair round her fingers.

'Well?' he prompted.

'I'm not sure where to begin. First of all though, I can't understand why you don't know my grandfather. If you're in charge of Jade Bay . . . ?'

'I know of him, but I never met him.'

'But how . . . '

'I'll tell you when I've heard your story. Then maybe we can fit them together. You mentioned your grandfather brought you up.'

'He and Grandma. My parents are dead. No, please don't be sorry, I'm not an Orphan Annie. Mum and Dad were wonderful, but they were away a lot. They ran a touring theatre group — and I mean touring — world wide. I went along a couple of times when I was young, but my main home was at Fred's and Emily's. Mum and Dad were killed in India. At the time, I didn't know the details, and my mother's parents simply slipped into my parents' rôle. I wasn't a deprived child in any sense. Even when Emily died, Grandad became my two parents. We had a great time except . . . ' Holly's brown eyes clouded. 'Except for boarding-school.'

'He sent you away?'

'He had to. I could understand that.' Holly was hotly defensive. 'I had to mix with my own age group, but I hated it. Looking back, it's difficult to believe that Grandad was so patient. I ran away so many times and begged to be allowed home. Eventually, he made a bargain with me — if I stayed at school, we'd take off every holiday. So that's what we did. We travelled everywhere, except America. I never knew why we didn't come out here.'

Jedd looked puzzled. 'Yet he did?'

'Not until I left college and started work.' She spoke quickly, rushing over the painful part. 'I last saw him a year ago at Heathrow Airport. He wanted to travel in the States. Since then, I've only had postcards. Mainly one-liners: 'great time', 'wish you were here' sort of thing. I had no idea he'd bought a charter-boat company, until — until — I heard he'd died.'

Her voice was so low that Jedd had to lean forward to hear her. He took her hands in his and held them until she smiled up at him, blinking back the tears. His warm firm grip was comforting.

She continued. 'His last card, some weeks ago, was somehow different from the others. He sounded excited and he was hinting that I should join him. He was going to Atlanta . . . '

Jedd's hands tightened suddenly, crushing her fingers until she cried out. Instantly, he relaxed his grip. 'Sorry. Finish your story.'

'There's not much else to say.' She looked down at her small hands, still imprisoned in his. Her fingers curled against his palm. 'By the time I had news of his death, he'd been buried. That's what's most painful, I think — not to have known, thinking he was alive and well. I didn't even know he had heart trouble and I can't imagine what he was doing on a solo boat trip.'

Her agonised, brown eyes stared at Jedd, and his heart twisted with pity for the young English girl. He put her fingers to his lips. 'You've had a tough time. Don't talk about it any more if you don't want to.'

She looked down. 'I'm sorry. I didn't mean to go all emotional on you. It's just — well — he'd always been there for me, and and that's why I have to do what he wants. And what he wants is for me to take over Jade Bay!'

'Which is where we came in.'

He released her hands, and the warm, protected feeling left her. 'Quite,' she said, desperately aiming at a brisk business-like tone. 'I understand. You just want the facts — about Jade Bay.'

He sighed and shook his head. 'Don't be so defensive. No, I don't just want the facts. I want to know how you feel about them. Haven't you talked to anyone back home? Someone as pretty as you must have a boyfriend, fiancé, partner? What does he say?'

'Er — yes, I do, sort of, but he's pretty busy at the moment.'

Jedd's snort of disbelief didn't lessen the hurt she'd buried at Dave's casual treatment of her problem. 'So, we all have to lose our grandparents,' he'd said. 'A fact of life, Holly.'

'But it's the most important thing in your life,' Jedd was saying. 'You can't simply just bury your grief. It's not natural.'

'Well, maybe it's the British way,' Holly rushed on, feeling vaguely disloyal to Dave. 'Anyway, Grandad left Jade Bay Charters to me. I can sell it, or run it for six months.'

Jade spread his hands. 'So, what's the problem? You've seen it. You can make up your mind pretty fast on that I imagine. I can't see you settling here for six months, winter coming up and all. I don't suppose your grandfather foresaw the seasons when he made the will. It doesn't seem very practical.'

Holly hesitated. Could she trust Jedd Rivers with the next bit of the story? She didn't have to tell him everything, and it couldn't do any harm. It may be useful to have one half of the partnership, at least, on her side.

'I can sell it, and thanks to you, it

looks in pretty good shape.'

'Thanks to Crystal, too,' he cut in sharply.

'Of course. Maybe you'd want to buy it with Crystal. But if I take it over as Grandad wanted, I get the chance to see the rest of the will.'

Jedd's eyes narrowed. 'The rest of it?'

'There's a second document which I get to see if I run Jade Bay myself for a specified period — minimum three months. If I sell, the Florida lawyer has instructions to destroy the second document.'

'That's pretty odd. Do you have any idea what's in the second document?'

Holly put her hands behind her back and crossed her fingers. 'No. It's probably just some made-up adventure game of Grandad's. We used to play them all the time. He had a great sense of humour. I had a magic childhood with him. I believe what he's done is a kind of 'In Memoriam,' that's all.'

'Maybe.' Jedd looked sceptical and picked up the bill. 'Puts a big responsibility on you, though.'

Holly reached for her purse. She and Dave always split the bill, but the American had a different view. He drew his brows together.

'Do you mind? I invited you, I pick up the tab.' A glint of amusement softened the electric, blue eyes. 'You're not the boss yet. As far as the bank's concerned, I still write the cheques. Crystal and I will need formal proof of all this, of course. Now, let's take a stroll by the water. It's early yet. What you've told me will take a while to sink in.'

'You haven't told me yet how you came to Jade Bay.' Holly was glad the meal was over.

They came out of the air-conditioned restaurant and her skin responded blissfully to the warm, pine-scented air. A wooden walkway ran the length of the building, ending in a flight of steps down to the beach. In a moment of release, Holly ran down the steps on to the soft sand. She took off her shoes, wriggling her toes in its grainy warmth.

Jedd relieved her of her sandals. 'Let me hold these — I can see you want to run right into the waves.'

Her eager face was turned to the ocean, but she stayed by him. 'I do, but not till you tell me about Grandad.'

They strolled towards the water's edge together, Holly acutely conscious of the tall American's easy, loping walk. In his hands, her flimsy sandals looked like doll's shoes.

'I told you. I'm sorry, but I never met him.'

A wave ran over her toes. It was cool, silky, delicious. A dramatic sunset was streaking the sky, touching her face and hair with deep gold. She turned to face him, her long, thick hair running like precious metal down her back. Jedd, darkly outlined against the sun, stared down at her. A murmuring edge of foam inched over his shoes, but he didn't move. Gently, he placed his hands on Holly's shoulders and drew her towards him, his fingers caressing the bare skin under her jacket.

Her voice seemed far away, thin against the rippling surf. She managed to say, 'So, if you didn't know my grandfather, what are you — and Crystal — doing at Jade Bay Charter Company?'

'That,' he murmured, 'is another story.' Then, slowly and deliberately and with tender delicacy, he lowered his lips to hers.

His touch on her shoulder should have alerted her. She should have moved away, not allowed his mouth to close on hers. She was sort of committed to Dave, wasn't she? Holly had always believed that commitment should be total. Emily and Fred had been her rôle model of a couple who'd happily spent their lives together with no covert, sideways glances on either side.

But Jedd's mouth on hers was sensationally breathtaking, obliterating logic, example, reason! After her small token movement of objection, the sweet pressure intensified as he drew her closer.

Giddy from the racing fire in her blood, Holly swayed when he released her. He touched her cheek, then laid his fingers across her mouth.

'I had to take my opportunity — before I turn into the hired hand at midnight! Come on, my feet are wet.'

He took her arm to walk her back to the shore line and Holly was staggered by his coolness. Her own lips were burning, her cheeks flushed. Jedd, on the other hand, was infuriatingly nonchalant. Confusion and frustration made her lash out.

'That's routine payment for dinner, is it?'

He dropped her arm, and there was a distinct cooling of the atmosphere.

'That remark doesn't deserve an answer.'

She tried to match the temperature. 'Thanks for the dinner. Now, if you'd just tell me how you and Crystal come to be running my business, I can go back to Silver Shores.'

Frostiness didn't come naturally to Holly, her natural persona being warm-hearted and generous-spirited. Her attempt at a sub-zero tone made Jedd break into laughter, and the deep music of the sound sent a hot prickle down her spine.

'Come off it, Holly. The high-and-mighty, Miss England performance doesn't wash. Bet you can't keep it up for more than five minutes. You're fire — not ice! You just showed it, so it's too late to back-track now.'

He sat down on the sand to remove his wet shoes and socks.

'OK, time to level with you, tell you my side of the set-up. But not with you standing over there, looking so cross.'

Taking her hand, he pulled her down to sit beside him. Her resistance ebbed away but she took care to leave a broad band of sand between them. As Jedd spoke, she didn't notice that the gap had narrowed!

'I'm a sort of impostor, you might

say.' Jedd stretched out comfortably on the still-warm ground, speaking slowly. 'I'm not a fisherman by trade, though I love the ocean. I was born here, but when I was young, my folks moved to Atlanta. That's where my home is now.'

'But how . . . ?'

He smiled at her, his shadowy profile still strong in the dusky light. 'You'll never hear the end if you interrupt. I came to Jade Bay as a favour to someone I love dearly.'

'Crystal?' she said flatly.

Jedd looked bemused. 'Crystal? No, I came here because my Aunt Cassie asked me to. Crystal had nothing to do with it, although she's the one you should make friends with if you want to find out about your grandfather. She and her boyfriend, Brett Dawson, were running the outfit before I appeared.'

Holly put her palms to her temples. Aunt Cassie? Brett Dawson? What had Fred got her into? Forgetting about the sandy gap she'd previously set between them, she collapsed against Jedd's strong shoulder. 'Please explain.'

He slipped an arm around her. 'Right. As simple as I can. Back in Atlanta, I run the family business, Rivers Finance. It's a complex organisation — high-pressure meetings, deals — all that. It's been tough lately. Let's just say I needed a complete break. So, when Cassie practically ordered me down here, I grabbed the chance because your grandad had been to see my Aunt Cassie.'

Swiftly, he pre-empted her startled question.

'He went to see her because, years ago, they were lovers.'

'What!' Holly shot away from him. 'That's impossible! I don't believe you. Fred and Emily . . . '

'Oh, it must have been well before your grandmother's time. They were very young, but from the little Cassie will tell me, it was a real Romeo and Juliet affair, star-crossed lovers and all that, except that they didn't die for love! Rich financier's daughter, Cassie

63

Rivers, couldn't be thrown away on a young pauper like Fred Peters! Just kidding,' he hastily added as he saw Holly's head go up. 'I don't know the ins and outs, but Aunt Cass never did marry. She had lots of chances, and she was a real beauty. She still is. Maybe that granddaddy of yours really had something!'

'Is that why he shied away from the States before? I'd no idea . . . '

'I don't suppose you did. Our relatives' younger lives are often closed books to us. It was a very long time ago.'

'So why did he go to see her, after so long?'

Casually, Jedd drew her back into the circle of his arm before he answered. It was quite dark, with only a faint sliver of moon showing that the beach was deserted. 'I'm not sure. Perhaps it was the pull of an old love — when he was on his own, with no more responsibilities. Perhaps Cassie will tell the story one day. For whatever reason initially,

Fred had visited and told her about the charter boats he'd bought her. She told me he was excited about something, but wouldn't tell her what, promising to go back to Atlanta soon with a great story for her. Seems he wanted a reliable lawyer in Florida, too. Cassie knows everyone from California to New York, so that was no problem. I guess he wanted to draw up the will.'

'Why didn't he tell me?' Holly cried. 'To think he was doing all this on his own!'

'He was probably enjoying himself. You said he loved games and adventure. Cass said he reminded her of an old-fashioned buccaneer. It didn't make much sense then, but I begin to see . . . '

'It's more than I do.'

'Let me finish. Weeks later, Fred phoned Aunt Cass. He was worried. Jade Bay was in deep debt — it had all gone wrong. He spoke of a partner who'd died. Maybe a partner with money, I don't know. But Fred knew

Cassie was a shrewd lady and he was desperate. Cass knew I was looking for a break, but I'm no beach lizard — I need a project. So she suggested I came down here to give a hand, and use my experience to try and turn things round.'

'Which you seem to have done.'

Jedd shrugged, but Holly felt the shift of muscles against her shoulder.

'It wasn't hard,' he said. 'There was great potential for a profitable outfit. Crystal and Brett have a cash-flow problem, but they're damned hard workers. Fred left them to it, off on some adventure of his own, obviously, but they got deeper into the mire. Only Crystal's local connections kept them afloat. They kept going on credit, but the crash wasn't far away. I came down and started work, hoping to meet Fred, but he never came back. I had to take charge, and wait around — until you showed up.'

'You knew I was coming?'

'Not exactly, but Crystal had heard

about the granddaughter, and Fred had hinted he'd asked you to come out. She and Brett want Jade Bay, but they've no money. Ironically, it's worth far more now than when Fred Peters was here. Brett's gone and got himself a high-paid construction job in Texas to raise funds. Your arrival, although it was half-expected, put a spanner in the works. It's quite a situation. Interesting, don't you think?'

'No, I don't. I think it's a terrible muddle.' She stood up. The moon had gone behind a cloud, and the beach was black. 'I'd like to go now. Thanks for telling me your side of the story.'

Jedd took her arm and guided her back to the walkway. 'First thing is to get to grips with the day-to-day running of the company. You can't afford to let go. We've come a long way, but there's a lot of competition out here. Crystal's excellent on the practical side, but sloppy on paperwork. It doesn't interest her.'

'Won't you be doing that for a while?' Holly tried to keep the hopeful note out of her vice.

'Heck, no! I've done what I came out for. I'll be heading back to Georgia, and the Rivers Corporation. I've had my break. It's been fun.' He sat down on the wooden steps and put on his socks and shoes.

Holly looked down at his thick, dark hair with a hollow feeling of desolation. What a fool she'd been. Of course he was rich — she only had to look at his car and his clothes to see that. Putting Jade Bay Charters on its feet was simply a holiday diversion for him.

Back in the parking lot, he opened the passenger door for her. She hesitated.

'Jedd — did you, have you put any money into Jade Bay?'

He paused, weighing his answer. 'There's a small amount of Rivers' money in there. Aunt Cass has a nose for a shrewd investment, and I've an idea she's not quite levelled with me. I think Fred told her more than she's telling me, for the moment.'

'So I don't own it outright?'

'Not quite,' Jedd said pleasantly as he closed the door.

4

Holly had plenty to think about on the short drive back to Silver Shores: the revelations about Grandad's past; Jedd leaving; Crystal's boyfriend and numerous other things to deal with. Right now, an ally would be good. Maybe she should ring Dave?

Just then, Jedd said, casually, 'I can't figure out your boyfriend. If you were my girl, nothing would keep me away. How could he let you do this alone?'

Perversely, Holly's thinking did a complete U-turn. 'I don't need him here. It's my affair.' Stung by Jedd's glance of disapproval, she added sharply, 'These are the nineties. Women can achieve without the obligatory male on hand.'

'I don't doubt it, but it would be more fun with someone.'

'Not necessarily.'

Yet, just at that moment, she was very glad that Jedd was with her. As the car drew up in the parking lot of Silver Shores, Holly automatically glanced up. The corner windows of her apartment were floor-to-ceiling plate glass and a second later, she clutched Jedd's arm.

'The lights are on in the sitting room. Look!'

'You must have left them on,' he said comfortingly. 'Easily done.'

'No. It was light when we left, and I definitely closed the doors on to the deck. Now they're wide open, and the curtains are blowing. Jedd!' Her voice rose to a startled pitch as a dark figure appeared on the deck, came to the rail, glanced down at the car and quickly disappeared.

Jedd killed the engine, but left the headlights on. He leaped out and sprinted to the main entrance.

'Don't,' Holly yelled. 'Come back, Jedd!'

But he was already climbing the stairs. She ran after him — he couldn't get in without a key. But then she slowed down — she didn't want him to get in until after the intruder had gone. Seconds later, Jedd came back down the stairs.

'Don't go in, Jedd. Call the police. There's nothing worth stealing in there. You might get hurt.'

He took the keys from her. 'Stay here. It's probably only a kid. There've been a few break-ins lately.'

'It didn't look like a kid. What if they have a gun, or a knife?'

'You've been watching too many movies! But keep back, just in case.' Jedd opened the door and went in.

Holly stayed close by him. 'It's my flat,' she muttered rebelliously, but her heart was in her mouth at the thought of a burglar cornered inside.

The apartment was open-plan and in a flash, Jedd had crossed the hall and living area, and was on the deck, leaning well over the balcony rail.

'He's gone!' he called down to her. 'I just saw him — he hopped on to the deck below, and off over the dunes. Probably came in that way, too. We'd never catch him.' He slid the gauze screen across the open window, then closed the glass doors. 'The locks have been forced.'

'I'd better call the police.' Holly glanced around the room.

'You should report it, though it looks as though we caught him in time. Everything OK in here? What about the bedroom?'

'I'll do that.' She rushed past him.

The king-sized bed dominated the entire room. Jedd followed, a twitch of amusement curving his lips, but his expression turned to concern when he saw her face. He went into the room and saw the reason.

'Ah! Whoever it was started in here and didn't care what sort of mess they made.' He looked at the chaotic jumble of clothes strewn across the bed. Every drawer had been emptied, every cupboard opened. 'Has anything been taken? Can you tell?'

Holly sat down on the bed. 'No, I don't think so. I haven't got much, and I didn't bring any jewellery or valuables.'

The only thing of value was in the sitting room. Swiftly, she made her way back there. The red folder was still in place, tucked behind some magazines on the bookshelf. But what possible value could that be to anyone but herself?

Jedd had followed her. 'I think he was looking for something specific. Any idea what that could be?'

'No. I've told you, there's nothing valuable here.'

He looked at her shrewdly, noting the defiant, yet puzzled look in her eyes. He had the feeling she wasn't telling him the whole truth, but decided not to press her on the matter — at least for the present!

'Shall I help you clear up?'

'No, please. It won't take long.' She desperately wanted him to go, to leave her to sort out her thoughts, but for some reason, he seemed reluctant to go.

'Will you be all right here tonight on your own? You should get that lock fixed. I'll send a security man to check the rest of them.'

'That's OK, I can manage. It's late. You ought to go. The janitor will take care of the locks, and I don't suppose there'll be a repeat visit tonight.'

'Shall I ring the police for you?' Jedd stepped towards her.

Holly felt a tingle at the base of her spine — a tingle of too high a voltage for comfort. She backed away. 'I'll do that. Goodnight, Jedd.' As he moved in closer and she saw the intention in his expression, she blurted out, 'And I've already paid for dinner.'

The look in his eyes turned to steel. 'I hadn't forgotten. I'll see you tomorrow. Goodnight, Miss Peters,' then he was gone . . .

She waited a few minutes, straining her ears to catch the sound of his car leaving, then she took the red file from the shelf behind her. She made a cup of coffee, carried it out on to the deck, and switched on the outside light. Savouring the warm, night air, she deliberately put off the moment, holding the file in her lap. It had remained unopened since she'd left London. Somewhere along the line, she'd decided that she shouldn't read the letter again until she'd located Jade Bay Charters, and was settled in the apartment. Now she put her cup down, and opened it.

The will was straightforward — simple, legal phrases, everything quite clear, if odd! She knew it by heart. The letter was a different matter. It was just as if Fred Peters were speaking directly to his granddaughter. Her fingers shook a little as she unfolded the single, closely-written sheet of foolscap.

My dearest granddaughter and friend, Holly, it began, *today I saw the doctor, and the news wasn't good. I had a stern instruction to put my affairs in order, so here goes.*

The letter was mainly about the past,

and the delight he and Emily had had in bringing up Holly. She read it sadly, but with gratitude for the love they'd given her. It was the last paragraph that went to the heart of her present situation.

. . . *explain the will. Indulge me, Holly, in this last game we'll play together. I'd hoped you'd be with me but, if you're reading this, well, it's not to be — you'll have to do with my spirit.*

Holly wasn't superstitious and certainly didn't believe in ghosts, but at that moment, she had a strong sense of her grandfather's presence, as she lifted her eyes to the black horizon. The curtains behind her stirred and settled, and she finished reading.

It's a treasure hunt and this is the first clue! Remember the ones in the old house and garden, with your gran? How you enjoyed them! This time, I'm sending you on a real beauty, but I want you to be sure you want to go ahead and learn the business through

Jade Bay Charters. Get to know the ocean. All those diving exams you took should pay off now. In three months, maybe six at the outside, you'll be ready. Then apply to Rechts and Kinskis for the second part of the will. There you'll find the real trail and all the other clues. Even then, you can still pack up and go home, sell Jade Bay and forget the whole thing. But I hope you won't. Perhaps that boyfriend you wrote about might help you. I have to warn you, there may be dangers, Holly. So guard the secret well, for others may be on the same trail.

There was no mention of Crystal or Brett, nor of Cassie or Jedd Rivers, only that Jade Bay was small, a bit run-down, but OK for its purpose. The letter ended with expressions of his deep love for her. Fred had never been a sentimental man, and the depth of his emotion surprised Holly.

She folded the paper, placed it to her lips, and then put it, together with the other documents, in a locked case in a cupboard in her closet. As she secured the apartment as best she could for the night, her mind was in a turmoil. It all sounded extraordinarily melodramatic! Treasure — dangers — secrets! It wasn't a surprise that her grandfather should turn it into a game.

It was no coincidence that his daughter, Holly's mother, had founded a theatre group, and it had been a deep disappointment to him that he'd never had the opportunity to join her and her husband. An original spirit . . . yes, Jedd's Aunt Cass had summed him up well — a buccaneer!

Holly moved restlessly around the apartment. Could the break-in have anything to do with the documents in the folder? But they were of no value. There was a copy of the will, the lease of the flat, the vehicle log — but did the intruder know that? No-one else in Florida would know about the strange two-part will — except Jedd, now.

The image of the intruder flashed into her mind, and she knew why it had been teasing her brain. Jedd had referred to 'he,' but Holly's impression had been that it was a female shape she'd glimpsed on the deck, outlined against the inside light. And what burglar would have left all the lights on? Unless he or she was sure the occupant was out of the way for the evening? Who were the 'others' referred to in Grandad's letter? Could it possibly be a team — Crystal Bankston and Jedd Rivers, for instance?

It was midnight — six o'clock in England. Not too early in the morning to phone her workaholic boyfriend. The ringing tone went on for a long time, but Dave's voice was wide-awake when he finally answered.

'Holly! It's great to hear you. How are things going? You've just caught me. My taxi's due any minute. I'm flying to the States this morning.'

'Dave!' Holly wasn't sure whether she was glad or sorry. 'Why didn't you let me know? I'll pick you up at the airport. Which one are you coming to?'

There was a pause, then Dave's voice, more hesitant. 'No, not Florida. I'm flying to New York. There's a deal there . . . look, here's the taxi . . . must dash. I'll ring you from New York.' Then, as an afterthought, 'I miss you, Holly.'

Then she phoned the police to report the break-in, but played it down. The last thing she wanted was a late-night visit from the sheriff's office! Then, thankfully, she sank into bed at last. It had been quite a day.

Next morning, as Holly was getting ready to go out, the phone rang. It was Anna Ramirez.

'Holly? This is Anna — yesterday, remember?'

'Of course.'

'Jamez and I would like to return your hospitality today. There's a wonderful Mexican restaurant outside San Maria. We'd like to take you to lunch.'

'Oh, there's really no need. I'm still in your debt. Besides, I've got an appointment today.'

'Are you free this morning? When's your appointment?'

'Er — evening actually.' Holly had always found it difficult to tell lies, even white ones, for social purposes.

'No problem then. We'll pick you up at eleven-thirty, and we've already been to the garage. Your truck's fixed and we can take you after lunch to pick it up.'

Holly started to protest, feeling she was somehow being taken over. It seemed as if her day was being organised by complete strangers. But Anna was not to be dissuaded.

'Please, you are a stranger to America. We like to help, make you welcome. You would do the same in England.'

Holly bowed to the inevitable, and was ready for them at eleven-thirty.

At least she was hungry on this occasion, and had no difficulty in enjoying the spicey Mexican food they ordered for her. They asked what she was doing in San Maria, and she told them she was working at Jade Bay

Charters but not, of course, that she owned it. They wanted to do some fishing, and were looking forward to scuba diving, too.

'How far do their charter boats go?' Jamez asked. 'We'd intended to go a little farther south, but if we can put some business your firm's way, we'd sure like to.'

'I don't know yet,' Holly confessed. 'I'll know more after this evening.'

'Don't worry, we're here for a while, and we'll make a start on the fishing tomorrow.'

'We're going to Mobile, in Alabama, this afternoon. It's not far — like to come along?' Anna asked casually, as they left the restaurant.

'Thanks, but I can't. I've got lots to do. Lunch was lovely. I appreciate it.'

They took her to the garage, insisting that they would be at Jade Bay Charters the following day to fix up the fishing, and to see her again to arrange a day out.

Holly was relieved to have the truck

back, although the mechanic was rather scathing about its age! Being without a vehicle in San Maria was no fun at all. She felt light-hearted as she swung the truck out on to the highway. At the nearest shopping mall, she stocked up with food, bought a swimsuit and a couple of cotton tops. She was beginning to enjoy herself, just as Fred Peters had known she would, in spite of the sadness in her heart as she still tried to come to terms with his death.

The euphoria lasted through the day. She tidied up the apartment, saw the janitor about the locks, and had a small snack at teatime.

'There's nothing wrong with this old truck,' she sang to herself, as she set off at seven o'clock for the waterfront. She felt reasonably confident of her approach at the meeting. Crystal would surely have had time to calm down. Holly was prepared to meet her more than halfway, in spite of the way she'd spoken about her grandfather.

The road down to the marina was

busy. At the top of the incline leading to the boardwalk, Holly pulled in to let a truck and trailer pass. Now that she knew where to look, she could see the Jade Bay Charters' berths. There seemed to be lots of people around. The boats must have just returned from the afternoon fishing trips.

Deciding to park down on the dock, she revved up the engine and pressed the accelerator. The truck shot forward, and Holly touched the brake. To her horror, nothing happened — except that the pick-up gathered speed at an alarming rate down the long slope. She stamped down hard, then pumped furiously on the brake pedal. Nothing! Trying not to panic, she took in the scene.

There were far too many people on the docks and boardwalk. Groups of tourists, strolling on the paved wharf in her path, glanced up in alarm at the vehicle speeding towards them. She realised that she couldn't slew the truck either right or left without hitting someone. Unless the brakes caught, there was only one way out.

The slope curved left to the carpark, which was crowded with people preparing to take their catches home for supper. If she kept straight on, the concrete apron led to the harbour, but it was her only route.

Pressing her hand hard down on the horn, she hurtled the last hundred yards down the slope. In vain, she stood on the brakes. Fred Peters' ancient vehicle shot into the air and began a slow and graceful descent into the water! As Holly struggled with the door handle, she automatically registered the scene around Sea Jade's berth. Jedd's tall figure stood out, astonishment on his face chased away by horror as he started forward.

Then, just before the truck hit the surface of the ocean, Holly saw Crystal's face; it expressed horrified fascination, but in her eyes there was a chilling something else — a glitter of pleased satisfaction.

5

Well before the truck hit the harbour floor, Holly was out of the door and kicking away from the falling vehicle. As long as she could get out, there was little danger. The water was comparatively shallow, no more than ten or twelve feet, and she was only under for a matter of seconds before surfacing, to the enthusiastic cheers of a crowd which had surged to the spot.

Feeling more foolish and embarrassed than anything, she swam to the nearest docking berth and hauled herself up on to a wooden jetty. Jedd was there to give her a hand, his expression a mixture of amusement and concern.

'That was a pretty dramatic entrance. I couldn't think of a better publicity stunt myself, although you should have had 'Jade Bay Charters' painted on the side of the truck. That'd have surely brought in some business.'

'It's not funny.' Holly wrung out her long hair.

'You're not hurt, are you? I could see you were almost out of the door before you hit the water. Just for a second, I was really worried, but you didn't panic. Well done, Holly. I'm afraid the old truck's a write-off. You shouldn't have been driving such a wreck.'

'It wasn't a wreck! The garage checked it over only last night.'

'Which garage? They couldn't have tested the brakes. I'll get straight on to them. Sheer incompetence.'

The crowd melted away, seeing that there would be no more excitement, and only Crystal and a tall, broad-shouldered man with thick, fair hair, remained on the jetty. Holly's shorts and shirt were already beginning to dry in the early evening warmth, but she felt uncomfortably clammy and salty.

Crystal stepped forward, and to Holly's surprise, all trace of animosity seemed to have vanished.

'Would you like a shower, Holly? I can lend you some dry things. They might be a shade too big, but that won't matter. There's a bathroom at the office. Oh, by the way, this is Andy Lawrence — our own full-time Cap'n Andy.'

'Hi, Holly,' Andy drawled as they all moved off towards the Jade Bay offices.

Holly turned eagerly to Andy. 'Did you know my grandfather?'

'Nope. I joined Jade Bay after Jedd here arrived. Crystal can tell you about him, though. She's told me plenty.'

They had arrived in the air-conditioned office. Jedd went into the smaller office to phone the garage, while Andy switched on the coffee machine. The two girls faced each other, Holly still wary in spite of Crystal's calmer manner.

There was a slight pause, then Crystal spoke. 'Look, Holly, I'm sorry about yesterday. I'd no call to speak about your grandfather like that. Jedd was right. All I can say is that I was

— upset yesterday — even before you appeared. I guess I'm missing Brett more than I realised.'

She held out her hand, and Holly took it, pleased, but not entirely convinced. She remembered the pleased expression on Crystal's face as the truck left solid ground. Still, a truce was better than yesterday's implacable enmity!

'OK, I'm sorry, too, for appearing out of the blue like that. Maybe I should have written first. I hope we can work together for Jade Bay.'

Crystal started to say something, but Jedd came back in, frowning.

'The mechanic at the garage swears that the brakes were good. He particularly checked, because of the age and general condition of the truck. I believe him — they've got a good reputation. He says the brakes couldn't possibly have failed unless they'd been tampered with.'

'That's impossible!' Holly burst out. 'Who would do such a thing? And why?'

Jedd shrugged. 'I've no idea, but that and last night's break-in . . . Wouldn't you say you've been mighty accident prone since you arrived in San Maria?'

The bubbling coffee broke the silence, and Jedd said decisively, 'They'll raise the truck as soon as possible. Maybe we'll find something then. Anyway, Holly, how about that shower? It's time we got down to business. You're in charge now.'

As she stood under the stinging spray a few minutes later, Holly began to wonder if she really wanted to be in charge!

The harbour débris sluiced from her skin, and her freshly-shampooed hair, tied back in a loose knot, did wonders for her morale. Crystal unexpectedly produced a stunning, turquoise T-shirt dress which set off Holly's new tan. She tried to push away the thought that someone might be deliberately trying to harm her, and resolved to enjoy the challenge of the meeting. If someone was trying to do her down, she was more than ever determined to succeed.

They sat round a small table in the main office. Andy served coffee and the others looked expectantly at Holly. She started a little hesitantly, but with growing confidence, as all three of them listened intently.

'I know my sudden appearance has been a bit of a shock. I apologise for that again, but my grandfather wasn't much of a conformist, and maybe a little of that's rubbed off on me. His legacy, Jade Bay Charters, was as much a surprise to me as to you, but I intend to do what he wanted. I am going to run it, and I am going to make a success of it. I hope it's with your help, but if any of you wants to pull out, I'll do it alone.'

Crystal remained silent.

'The most amazing thing so far,' Holly continued, tapping the papers before her, 'is what a buoyant, thriving operation this is. You must have worked incredibly hard because, you see, my grandfather indicated that it was, to put it mildly, in a poor way.'

'It was. I told you.' Crystal couldn't be silent on this point.

'I understand that now,' Holly conceded. 'I'm grateful, and I don't want to interfere in any way with what's going on now.'

'But you are staying?' Andy queried.

'Yes, I have to. No, I want to, but, and I'd like to hear what you think about this, I propose to develop my own side of Jade Bay.'

Holly was firm, but friendly still, and Jedd, tipping back in a chair which looked far too small for him, knew that his first impression had been correct. There was a streak of steel beneath the luscious and appealing exterior of Holly Peters. He wished he'd met Fred. Now he resolved to put a visit to Aunt Cass high on his agenda when he was back in Georgia.

Holly was now running through the trading figures, showing a sharp grasp of business details. She certainly wasn't just a pretty face. He was aware of her keen analysis.

'So business looks good, but I know the season's a short one. Trade drops off in winter, but one of the things I'd like to do is to beat that trading drop-off,' Holly said.

'I think we could mount package deals, liaise with motels, restaurants, airlines even, to promote San Maria — and Jade Bay Charters particularly, of course — as an international tourist attraction.'

Crystal and Andy looked a bit stunned, and it was Jedd who said lazily, 'Ambitious, Holly. And you'd need a lot of finance for that sort of advertising. Usually folk come to San Maria as part of their own trip.'

'There's no reason why San Maria shouldn't be the main focus. As to money, I don't agree. I've got contacts in Britain — travel companies I've worked for. I'm sure they'd be interested.'

'But we only have fishing to offer,

and winter weather can be rough sometimes.'

'That's a chance we'll have to take. And you're wrong. You can offer underwater sports — snorkelling and scuba diving.'

'We already do some of that.' Crystal was defensive.

'You were all for directing me towards your rivals yesterday when you thought I wanted snorkelling,' Holly pointed out.

'That was different. I wanted . . . ' She stopped and bit her lip.

Wanted to be rid of me, Holly thought, mentally finishing Crystal's sentence.

'Let's face it,' Jedd said, 'we've never done much on those lines.'

'That's because we had to build up the charter-fishing side. It was so hopeless . . . ' Crystal flushed.

Holly spoke soothingly. 'I know, I know. You've worked wonders, you and Andy. So, I want you to continue being totally in charge of the fishing. I'll build up the snorkelling and diving — particularly the latter. Divers in the UK would give their eye teeth to explore these beautiful waters. There are a lot of wrecks, apart from the fish.'

'You've done much diving?' Jedd was casual.

'Quite a bit.'

'You can't take parties down without certification.'

'Is British Sub-Aqua Club Instructor level acceptable?'

The silence spoke volumes.

'Pretty impressive,' Jedd said.

The meeting came to a natural end. Holly had suggested a profit-sharing scheme for Crystal and Andy instead of straight salaries, so they had plenty to think about. Holly was to start work immediately, and she suggested a further, formal meeting at the end of the week, after meeting all the part-time employees.

'I'll drive you home,' Andy offered.

Jedd stepped in quickly. 'It's OK, Andy, I've already arranged to do that.

We'll call in at the garage on the way.'

Holly, mouth open to accept Andy's offer, snapped it to again. Attractive as Jedd was, he did have a tendency to take over, although, admittedly, he'd been pretty unobtrusive during the meeting.

'Another time?' Andy said, his eyes openly admiring.

'Thanks, but I hope to have a car as soon as possible.' Holly deliberately misunderstood. There were enough complications in this scenario, without getting involved with Cap'n Andy!

'Can I have a word?' Crystal lingered by the door.

'Sure. Thanks for the loan of the dress. I'll wash it, and return it tomorrow.'

'No, no, keep it. It looks better on you anyway. I need to lose a bit of weight. What I want to ask is whether Brett can come back? If you're thinking of expanding, maybe he can help. He's an experienced diver, too.'

Aha! Holly thought there'd been

something behind Crystal's comparatively model behaviour. She wanted her boyfriend back on the scene. Holly wasn't yet prepared to trust Crystal, even Jedd for that matter, although in the morning light, her suspicions about his involvement in last night's break-in had seemed far-fetched. Crystal was still an unknown quantity, and Brett would be her ally. Crystal on her own was formidable enough — she'd seen that yesterday. She temporised. 'Well, shall we see how it goes? Give me a day or two to settle in?'

Crystal's scowl was controlled just too late for it not to show in her eyes, but she said mildly, 'OK — and Holly, I'll talk to you about your grandad any time you want.'

'I'd like that. Thanks.' Holly smiled. But she wasn't to be bribed. Crystal would have to prove whose side she was on first.

Jedd was waiting for her outside, leaning against the side of his silver sports car, talking to Andy. His keen, blue-eyed look had a strange affect on her, and she thought it was a good thing he'd be going back to Atlanta. She was thinking about him far too much!

They said their goodbyes to Andy, who was taking the Texans on a night-fishing trip, and headed towards Silver Shores. The air was warm, the breeze delicious, the coast and sea sensationally colourful. Holly leaned back and closed her eyes.

'Tired?' Jedd queried.

'No, not a bit.'

'No ill effects from the ducking?'

She laughed. 'You know, I'd quite forgotten that.'

'You've got guts, Holly Peters.' He put a hand on her knee, and she held her breath. 'You were pretty good at the meeting, too. Are English girls usually so full of surprises?'

'Haven't you met many?'

'Certainly not many like you,' he said, pulling up in the parking lot of a mall.

'Why've we stopped?'

'You're free tonight?' was his answer.

'Well . . . '

'Good. If you haven't tasted fresh Gulf Bay mullet, you've missed out on one of life's treats. I'm going to cook supper for you — at your place. I want to check your new locks, too. You stay here. Shan't be long.'

He strode off towards a fish market store before she could protest. There he was again, making her decisions for her! Still, red mullet with Jedd was a more attractive proposition than a boiled egg with American TV. So she decided she'd let herself be ordered around — on this occasion!

Holly didn't regret it for a minute. It turned out to be a wonderful evening. Jedd was an accomplished cook, grilling the fresh mullet and serving it with a delicately-flavoured sauce. They ate outside on the deck, with the ocean murmuring almost beneath them. Jedd had bought a fabulous, white wine, and they lingered over the meal.

The atmosphere was light-hearted, with no mention of Jade Bay, or Fred Peters' strange legacy. Holly felt totally relaxed, and when Jedd finally left, she responded to his light, farewell kiss. For a second, she felt him hesitate, and sensed they were on a knife-edge of tension for the only time in the evening. But he lifted his head and drew back.

'Goodnight, Holly. It's been quite an evening.'

She had to ask. 'When are you going back to Atlanta?' She had an excuse. 'Crystal wants Brett to come back, and I thought, with you gone . . . '

He touched her cheek. 'My flight's booked for tomorrow.' A numb sensation clutched her heart, then receded, as he added, 'but I think I'll postpone it for a while. I'd rather like to stay here, to see you settled in. Rivers Incorporated can spare me a few more days. Tomorrow, I'll show you the snorkelling reefs.'

Holly had always loved the ocean, rarely living far from the coast, although during her last year, she'd had to make do with the Thames as her nearest stretch of water. Born in The Seychelles during one of her parents' forays to unlikely venues, she'd lived afterwards with Emily and Fred in Scotland, and Northern England, getting to know the storm-battered coasts of the North. At boarding-school, on the south coast, diving was the sports teacher's great passion. He'd passed it on to the young Holly, and she'd rapidly progressed up the ladder. Fred had encouraged her, although he couldn't swim himself!

Holly always put great faith in Fred, but even he couldn't have known she'd end up putting her diving skills to the test in the Gulf of Mexico. Or could he?

Next day, snorkelling round the reefs out in the bay with Jedd, she felt a strong sense of her grandfather's spirit, floating on top of the clear, emerald water. It was almost like clues along a trail — a sense of going in the right direction.

When they finally surfaced for a last

time, Jedd took the boat around the reefs used by Jade Bay for snorkelling parties.

'The reefs are mainly man-made,' he told her. 'The ocean bottom is pure sand here, so we have to create our own reefs to attract the fish — and the tourists.' He laughed.

'How can you make a reef?'

'Easy. That one out there is made purely of old car wrecks — all cleaned up to high standards to avoid pollution, but wrecks nevertheless. That particular one was made by Jade Bay's owner.'

'Grandad?'

'No. He'd never have managed it in the short time he was here. The previous owner, apparently.' He turned the boat towards the harbour. 'You must meet the rest of the staff and bone up on your deep-sea diving skills. Time to get back to work, Holly.'

'Hasn't this been work?'

He gave her a long look. Her hair, fast drying in the sun, hung long and sleek around her shoulders, her white swim suit emphasising her tanned legs. 'If this is work,' he said softly, 'it's not the kind I do in Atlanta!'

Jedd had put into words exactly how Holly felt at the end of the week. It seemed she'd been in San Maria for ever, had always lived and worked out of doors, alongside the ocean. She could no longer imagine a Tube train or an overcoat. Her life was now so different from London.

From Dave, in New York, there was a deafening silence, but Holly was guiltily aware that he'd almost slipped her mind. Jedd had said nothing about Atlanta, and, together with Crystal and Andy, had taught Holly all she needed to know about the basic running of Jade Bay. She was confident she could easily manage three — six — even twelve months. Such was her optimism after only seven days!

Crystal was helpfulness itself, and although they hadn't yet had the talk about Fred, it was because they'd all been too busy. Next month, October, the heat would lessen, and the month-long, famous fishing rodeo would take place, bringing a lot of business for the charter-fishing side of the company. Holly planned to start work on the diving promotion the following week.

She presided at the weekly meeting with calm authority. In addition to Jedd, there were two students; Kate, an Australian, and Pete, from a local, fishing family. Holly had invited any one of the casuals who was interested to come to the meetings.

Jedd sat next to her. He'd been her constant instructor by day, but since the night he'd cooked supper for her, she hadn't seen him in the evenings. She knew he'd taken out three night-fishing parties and the rest of the time was flying by. Throughout the meeting, he seemed pre-occupied, his blue eyes hooded. His mouth, usually so relaxed, looked tight.

Holly concentrated on the others. 'I'm really pleased with this first week. You've all been great,' she concluded after a survey of the following week's busy schedule. 'Thanks, everyone.' The phone interrupted her. 'Well, let's leave it at that for now. It's getting late.'

Crystal picked up the phone. 'Jade Bay . . . oh, it's you. Yes, he's here. Now? OK. Yes, fine — and you?' She passed the receiver to Jedd. 'Noreen.'

A flicker passed over his face. 'I'll take it in the other office.'

Holly felt a strange pang of unease. Through the glass door, she could see Jedd speaking rapidly. Occasionally, his raised arm would chop through the air. She couldn't take her eyes off his hunched shoulder muscles.

'Come on,' Crystal called out from the door. 'The others have gone on. You promised us a drink.'

'Coming. What about Jedd?'

'Oh, he'll be hours yet if Noreen's anything to do with it.'

'Noreen?'

'Noreen Reynolds, the singer. Surely you've heard of her — The Singing Southern Belle from Georgia. A real TV hit in this neck of the woods. She's Jedd's lady! Can't wait to get him back, I'll bet.'

They saw Jedd put down the phone, and as he came into the room, Holly's heart did a swallow dive to her feet. She knew from his face exactly what he was going to say.

'Aren't you coming for a drink?' Crystal asked him.

'No thanks. There's a plane to Atlanta tonight. I'll be catching it. The holiday's over. I'm sure you'll get by without my help, Holly.' And with the briefest of nods, he left the building.

6

Holly's sense of loss was acute for the first few days after Jedd left, but life at Jade Bay was full and hectic and she often worked on in the evenings. The hurt of his abrupt, unfriendly departure wasn't lessened by his brief and formal telephone call from Atlanta a few days after he left San Maria. It was quite late when he rang; Holly, exhausted by a full day, was nearly asleep.

'Holly? Jedd Rivers.'

She snapped on a bedside light.

'Did the report on the truck come through? The garage promised it for today.'

'Yes, it did.'

He sounded quite different from the relaxed Jedd she'd known in San Maria. He was crisp, efficient, to the point of being curt.

'Well?'

There was impatience in his tone and she didn't like it.

'Holly? You sound half-asleep. The truck? The brakes?'

'Not very conclusive, I'm afraid. Apparently the brake fluid had gone, and the cable was twisted, but whether it was just the impact, or the tide . . . they didn't raise it for a few days.'

'You're not using it, I hope?'

''Course not. I've bought a car.'

'Where from?'

'Andy recommended a dealer. Look, Jedd, it's late, and it's not really any of your business any more. I'm quite capable of sorting things out myself. You have money in Jade Bay so, of course, I'll keep you up to date, but . . . ' She hesitated, still hurt by his business-like approach. 'My personal life's my own.'

She could sense anger on the silent line, then icily and uncharacteristically, he said, 'Very well, Miss Peters, if that's how it's to be.'

'Yes, it is. Goodnight, Jedd.'

She put the phone down, punched her pillows, and buried her head under the duvet. She wasn't going to cry — there was too much else to do . . .

Jade Bay Charters hit a small boom in trade. The diving venture showed some success, but so far, it was mainly locals and passing tourist trade. It was too late in the season to cast the net wider, but she had made her plans for next season. She had not thought of returning to London. It seemed to her now as a distant city on another planet!

The annual San Maria Fishing Rodeo meant lots more charter trips, and Jedd's absence was felt. Holly was forced to agree with Crystal. Another hand was needed and she thought it might just as well be Brett Dawkins, who knew the business. Crystal blossomed at the thought of his return, and worked harder than ever.

Holly realised that much of their success came from Crystal's local connections and knowledge, although she herself was responsible for bringing in some business, through Jamez and Anna Ramirez. A party of their relatives was due to arrive to join them for a week or two, and they had booked daily charters and diving trips through Jade Bay.

Crystal and Andy were scheduled to take out a Ramirez party for a night trip, and in a rare lull between day and evening work, Holly and Crystal shared coffee and sandwiches while they waited for the tourists to arrive. Andy was on board Sea Jade II, checking out the equipment.

It was a wonderful evening. A long, concrete bridge, spanning the water-ways, glowed an almost surreal pink, softening its hard contours.

'Wonderful,' Holly breathed, her face touched by the rosy colours.

Crystal looked at her watch. 'It should hold for half an hour. Just right for the start of the sunset sail.'

The silence between them was companionable, and for the first time, Holly felt comfortable enough with

Crystal to broach the subject of her grandfather.

'You didn't like Fred much, did you?'

Crystal sighed. 'That's not true. Oh, I know I called him an old fool, and I'm sorry for that. Actually, I thought he was great when we first met him — in a restaurant. It was busy, and we had to share a table. He was real entertaining; been just about everywhere in the States and all over Europe, too. We invited him back to the apartment for a drink, and he promised to try out a Jade Bay fishing trip next day.'

'And did he?'

'Sure. He knew nothing about fishing, but he enjoyed it — spent most of the time talking to folks. That's what he seemed to enjoy best. He got to know lots of people on the wharf. Everyone thought he was cute — even kinda lovable. I guess the trouble started when Juan arrived on the scene.'

'Juan?'

'Juan Santos, he called himself. He was a real eccentric! He and Fred met in a bar, and from then on, Fred seemed almost as weird as Juan. Juan lived in an old shed on the quay, and spent his time poring over maps and old books. He wouldn't move into Silver Shores, although Fred was always asking him to. Juan said they'd get him there, whoever they were. He was paranoid, and hardly ever left the shed. Then suddenly, he and Fred had bought Jade Bay Charters, and Juan moved into Pelican Venturer. That's the original, old tub Jade Bay was founded on. Jedd soon sent it out to the scrap heap.'

'What happened to Juan? Is he still around?'

Crystal looked astonished. 'Juan? He's dead, of course.'

'Dead? But how?'

'Didn't your grandad tell you anything?' Crystal's eyes narrowed.

'Not much.' Holly was cautious. 'He was about to send for me.'

'He should have sent you the newspapers.'

'Newspapers?'

'Yeah. *Hero from Britain Risks Life for Friend — In Vain*. Something like that. I've got it somewhere. Hey, here's the Ramirez crowd. They're early. Must go.'

'Crystal! What about Fred?'

'Tell you later.'

'No, now! Andy's on board, and he'll cope. Tell me.'

'OK, OK. Those two — er — Juan and Fred — were crazy. Kept taking out Pelican, and staying away for days. We warned them the boat was dicky, but they took no notice. They went out, a storm blew up, Juan fell overboard, Fred jumped in after him . . . '

'But he couldn't swim.' Horror-stricken, Holly put her hand on Crystal's arm.

'I know that. He knew that. Still, he went in. Look, Holly, I gotta go. You, too. They're all on board.'

'Finish the story, please. As we go.'

Crystal picked up her bag and boarding schedules, and they went out together. She spoke rapidly. 'That's it. The coastguards found them hours later, clinging to Pelican Venturer. Your grandad had held Juan up all that time. He could have got back into the boat, but Juan, although he was still alive, was too weak. He died later in hospital, and your grandad was with him the whole time. After Juan's death, he just got odder and odder. He left us to it much more, not that he was ever much help. But then, it's all in the past now.'

They reached the docking bay. 'But I still don't understand . . . '

'Holly, look, I'm sorry, but we've a job to do. Business — remember?'

There seemed to be dozens of Mexicans on Sea Jade II, but when Crystal took a head count, there were only six, including Jamez. One young man, taller than the rest, was introduced as Jamez' nephew.

Crystal stared hard at him. 'You've been out with us before.'

'Only once,' he replied.

His white teeth flashed, but the frown

didn't fade from Crystal's eyes. Holly, casting off the moorings, hadn't heard. As she waved Sea Jade off into the sunset, she was wondering whether Crystal had told her everything.

★　★　★

By the end of the Fishing Rodeo, Holly had completed her first month at Jade Bay. Brett Dawkins, a burly, blond six-footer, had arrived the day after the Ramirez' night trip, and proved a great asset right away.

It was all going far better than Holly could possibly have hoped. Jedd had made a couple of brief phone calls to the office, and Holly had returned weekly figures. She buried deep the hurt of his indifference and got on with the job.

Dave was back in London, now commuting regularly to New York. He spoke vaguely of flying down one week-end from Manhattan. Holly was pleased that he never turned up. She just couldn't visualise him in San Maria, gutting, cleaning and bagging the tourists' fish catches!

Once or twice, she'd been out for a drink with Andy, usually after the day's work. Holly would not admit that she was lonely. Everyone was so friendly and kind and the Ramirez took it upon themselves to keep an eye on her.

Andy asked her out to dinner to celebrate the end of the Rodeo, and her first month. She accepted but managed to arrange it so that Crystal and Brett joined them, which hadn't been Andy's intention at all!

In spite of that, the evening went well. They ate at The Back Porch, a restaurant with a wide deck, open to the ocean, only a mile away from Silver Shores. Afterwards, they walked back along the beach to Holly's apartment for coffee. At the apartment, she opened a bottle of wine with the coffee. Andy had coffee, then left. He was driving, and had an early start in the morning.

Suddenly she felt enormously tired, and wondered how long Brett and Crystal intended to stay.

'One more drink, then we'll be going.' Brett answered the unasked question.

'I think I've had enough,' Holly protested, but Brett had already pushed another glass into her hand.

She smiled up at him. What a tower of strength he was proving to be — and Crystal, too, after their unpromising start. She couldn't have managed without them, she thought, almost affectionately, as she looked at them. The music was soft and beguiling. Her head felt a little fuzzy.

'So,' Crystal asked, 'you going to stay on here?'

'Of course. Hasn't this month proved I can do it? With your help, of course,' she added quickly.

'Then what — just how long are you here for, Holly?'

'Three months.' She stopped. They had no idea about the terms of her grandfather's will. She'd forgotten that.

'Just three months?'

'Well — I don't — I'm not sure. Why?'

Crystal looked at Brett, who frowned at her, but she burst out, 'We have to know where we stand, Brett and I. Fred always promised that we'd be rich. We thought he meant Jade Bay Charters, but one night, on Pelican, Juan and Fred were talking — they were real excited. I heard them mention gold, artefacts, treasure. But as soon as they saw me, they clammed up. There's more to this than you're telling us, I reckon.'

Holly's head ached. That last drink must have been strong. She heard herself say, 'Maybe there is — but, I can't tell yet. All I have to do is run Jade Bay for three months — successfully. Then, we'll see.' She yawned hugely. The urge to go to sleep was overwhelming. 'I'm sorry, I don't mean to be rude, but . . . '

'Come on, Crystal.' Brett hauled her

up, and literally tucked her under his arm. 'Holly's whacked. See you tomorrow.'

That was the last thing Holly remembered of that evening, but afterwards, she was to recall that it was from there that things began to go wrong.

7

The locals had warned Holly about the weather in the Fall, but the sun had shone so benignly since she'd arrived, it was difficult to believe it would ever change. Just to teach her a lesson, the smile on the face of San Maria abruptly turned into a snarl. She woke one morning to grey skies and lashing rain; the temperature had dropped, and the view from the deck had totally changed. Instead of soft, emerald calm, angry, white-topped pewter lashed outside, flinging salt spray on to the windows.

At Jade Bay, Brett and Crystal were checking rods and equipment, philosophical about the change.

'Unpredictable, this time of year. Could be gone by sunset.' Brett was laconic.

'It's the hurricane season still,' Crystal said. 'Could be the end of the month before we're completely clear. Anything can happen.'

'What about the trips booked for today?'

'If the customers want to go out, we go. Today isn't too bad, but it's blowing up a bit and no good for weak stomachs. At a certain point, we don't go at all, of course, but there's a long way to go before we reach that.'

The quays became busy again as the rain eased off. Brett and Crystal went to greet the clients, but Holly's snorkelling party had to be cancelled, and she worried about the dive which was booked the next day. It was the third of a set of six, all booked and paid for.

Jamez Ramirez and his nephew, Paulo, would be in the party, and she and Brett hoped to go six miles out into the bay to the wreck of a liberty ship, about fifty feet down. There was nothing she could do about the weather, only be patient and hope for clearer skies tomorrow.

On the quay, Brett prepared to cast off Sea Jade I. The ocean beyond the sand bar looked choppy. She followed the plunging progress of the boat through binoculars until it was out of sight, and tried to push away a sense of foreboding.

It turned out that her misgivings were justified. Sea Jade I was due to return by noon, but by half past one, there was no sign of her. The weather had worsened, but a few stalwarts, booked for the two o'clock trip, had already gathered by the docking berth. Andy arrived to take out the afternoon trip.

'Where's Sea Jade? She should have been in a couple of hours ago. Not that any sane person should want to go out in that lot.'

'She went out this morning. I've tried to raise her on the radio, but it's either dead or full of static.'

Andy crossed to the communications console, keyed in the code and listened. He was rewarded with a burst of static, then dead silence.

'What is it?' Holly caught his anxiety.

'Radio's out. I'll check Central Control. There should be some boats in the area.'

'Not many went out this morning. There aren't many empty spaces on the dock. You don't think anything serious could have happened?'

'Shouldn't think so. They're not far out. Ah — I think I have someone. Sweet Jody's out there.'

Holly listened to the exchange between Andy and the captain of Sweet Jody. Half of it she didn't understand, but it seemed that Sea Jade was wallowing at anchor, with engine failure — and no radio!

'It's impossible.' Andy was incredulous. 'Engine and radio equipment are brand new — computer driven. They can't fail!'

'It seems they have. What do we do now?'

Holly felt helpless. Nothing had prepared her for this. The smiling idyll of the last few weeks was all of a sudden showing a grim face. But Andy took charge. Without losing one jot of his easy, laid-back style, he directed a rescue operation to tow Sea Jade I back to berth, leaving Holly to direct the two o'clock customers to Sea Jade II.

But bad news travels fast and most of those waiting by the Jade Bay kiosk had drifted off. Those who'd already paid wanted their money back. Rumour was that a Jade Bay Charter boat had foundered.

Paulo Ramirez was waiting to meet his father and uncle, and wanted to know if it was true that Sea Jade was sinking.

'Of course not,' Holly replied. 'She'll be in shortly.'

She turned up two hours late, ignominiously towed by Sweet Jody and a motorised catamaran which had been in the area. The customers were disgruntled. Several of them had been sea-sick, and a refund didn't pacify them. Holly did her best to make up, offering hot coffee and sandwiches, and a promise of a free trip later in the week.

Brett, usually so phlegmatic, stormed off to ring the engine and radio manufacturers. Jamez Ramirez, and his brother, Luiz, tried to help Holly by making light of it.

'The dive's still on?' Jamez asked.

'Well . . . ' Holly looked uncertain.

'I shouldn't,' Andy put in, 'not in these conditions.'

'The forecast's good for tomorrow.' Jamez zipped up his anorak. 'I hope you aren't going to let us down, Holly. Paulo's been looking forward to it. He so enjoyed the last couple of times.'

'We'll see what the weather's like,' Holly replied.

Although the sun shone the next day, and the wind had died, Andy warned her that the sand would be stirred up, so the sea'd be cloudy and probably silted up round the wreck. It was Jamez who persuaded her to proceed as planned, and although it wasn't a total disaster, Andy was right. The previous day's storms had churned the fine sand, and it was impossible to see much around the sunken liberty ship.

At the end of the dive, there was an unspoken air of dissatisfaction amongst the clients. The usual elation upon surfacing was totally absent, as they glumly peeled off their dry-suits. To top it all, the sun disappeared, and the evening breeze, often balmy in October, turned distinctly unfriendly, and the boat ride back was uncomfortably choppy.

'Come and have supper with me — you look really down.' Andy put his arm around Holly's shoulders as she prepared to lock up the Jade Bay offices for the night.

For a moment, she was tempted. It would be nice to forget about the setbacks for an evening, but Andy was a shade too attentive, and Holly couldn't help knowing she attracted him. In different circumstances, maybe! But she just didn't think it would be a good idea just now.

'Not tonight, thanks. I'd be miserable company. Let me have a good solo, misery wallow. I'll be better in the morning, and I've loads of paper work to do.'

Andy looked doubtful. 'Sure you'll be OK? I could come back with you. Cook you supper?'

Holly wondered if she looked ill-nourished. The American concensus appeared to be that she needed feeding all the time.

'No, really,' she said firmly, but tempered the refusal with a warm smile. Even that was a mistake, she thought ruefully, as she saw hope rekindled in Andy's eyes.

The evening stretched endlessly. It got dark earlier now. The summer season was over, and there was a gap before the snowbirds from the north, as the locals called the out-of-season tourists, arrived to enjoy the winter in temperate Florida. Not many of the apartments were occupied. When Holly went out on to the deck, only a few lights glimmered in the blackness. She shivered, and went back in. She tried the endless TV channels, and hit the weather forecaster's dire warnings!

'Hurricane Pat, moving up through the Caribbean, now over Northern Cuba. It's a weak system at present, but signs are it could be a big one. We'll keep you posted. Meanwhile South Florida, watch out for the storm warnings.'

That's all we need, Holly thought. Hurricane Pat bursting over the Gulf. Holly got up to look at a map of the Americas on the wall. Cuba looked a reassuring distance away. Just then, the phone rang. As always, Jedd came into her mind. She couldn't help it — it seemed he was never far from her mind, though she would have tried to deny it if anyone had asked.

'Holly, Anna Ramirez. Jamez tells me the dive didn't go too well and you looked a bit down. Like to come over for a while?'

'That's kind, but I'm really tired,'

Holly answered truthfully. 'I've got paper work, too, so another time, maybe. Thanks.'

They chatted for a while. Anna was worried about Hurricane Pat. She'd been in a hurricane before, and knew from her own experience the damage to life and property which could be caused. Holly tried not to listen too hard, and was very glad when Anna put the phone down.

It rang again immediately. This time it must be Jedd.

'Miss Holly Peters?' The voice had a very pronounced Southern drawl, not Jedd's. 'Owner of Jade Bay Charter Company?'

'Yes. Speaking.'

'You got my letter? OK if I see you tomorrow? I phoned your office just now and got your answering machine which gave this number.'

'I'm sorry. What letter?'

As far as she knew, there'd been nothing unusual in the post, although the events of the last few days had claimed most of her attention. She'd flicked through the mail only briefly that morning. An expression of annoyance clicked down the line. 'There's not much point writing to you folk if you don't read your mail. It's not very businesslike, Miss Peters.'

'I've been ... busy. Is there a problem?'

'Maybe. The letter explains it, but there's been a complaint about the Jade Bay reef — the one made from auto wrecks. It's alleged that proper environmental procedures weren't observed. That could cause long-term pollution.'

'But that was laid down before I came. Well before my grandfather bought the business even.'

'You're the owner, so you're responsible. We'd like to go out and take a look anyway. Always have to act on a public complaint.'

'Who ... ' she began but knew he wouldn't tell her. She changed her query to, 'What'll happen?'

'We'll send divers down. You should

have checked it out, of course, but seeing you're new, we won't be too hard on you. If anything's amiss, you'll just have to raise the wrecks, steam clean them, and put them back. That's all.'

'All!' Holly's voice rose. 'What'll that cost?'

'Good few dollars, I expect. But don't worry at this stage. Mebbe nothing to it. I'll be round first thing tomorrow.'

'No, I may not be there. You can talk to Crystal Bankston or Brett Dawkins.'

It was the last straw. Holly had no clue about United States' environment laws, what rights she had, or what mistakes had been made. There was Rivers' money in Jade Bay — as part owners, they'd be part responsible. She dialled Jedd's number . . .

* * *

'Didn't you ask whom he was representing?' Jedd leaned forward, resting his elbows on his desk.

'No, I didn't. I — I was taken by surprise.'

Holly had left San Maria at dawn and on a clear freeway, she'd made it to Atlanta by eleven o'clock. Jedd met her in the palatial reception area of an imposing, down-town skyscraper, given over entirely to Rivers' Finance. It was a much bigger operation than she'd imagined.

Jedd was another surprise. She hardly recognised him. In a lightweight, grey suit, white shirt and dark tie, he was clothed to fit his executive authority. His wavy hair was trimmed much closer to his scalp than she remembered. He looked older, very assured, dominant.

Her heart gave the familiar lurch when he came to meet her. He said he was pleased to see her, but the greeting had been formal and the expression in his clear, blue eyes hard to fathom. He looked at her hard, and Holly wished she'd worn something more suitable for the executive suite.

'I think someone is trying to cause

problems for you at Jade Bay.' He leaned back. 'There are just too many coincidences. Any ideas?'

'No.' Holly didn't voice her suspicions about Crystal, and by association, Brett. She had absolutely no proof, just a feeling of uneasiness which, she had to admit, could easily stem from Crystal's initial hostility.

Jedd glanced at his watch. 'I've got a meeting right now. I tried to cancel, but there wasn't time. Shouldn't take long. Half an hour — then I'll take you to lunch.'

'But I've got to get back — and — er — I'm not dressed . . . '

She babbled inanely. Jedd's tall figure was having a brain-scrambling effect on her. He got up, put his hand on her shoulder, and squeezed it gently.

'Don't be silly. We'll go for a hamburger, if you'd prefer it!' His eyes mocked her gently. 'Anyway, Aunt Cass wants to meet you, so don't you dare go away. I'll send coffee along, and there are newspapers and magazines in the racks.'

When he'd gone, Holly exhaled a sigh of relief. She felt secure when he was around, but he made her nervous, too, in an exciting and unsettling kind of way. Coffee appeared within minutes. Joanne, Jedd's secretary, introduced herself, and brought in some new magazines.

'Help yourself.' The tall, leggy brunette was city-office smart, but friendly and smiling, and Holly settled back to relax after the long drive.

The deep, leather chair and the quiet office were so comfortable that after a while, her eyes began to close and her head to nod. A delicious languor spread through her — Jedd was in charge! He'd take care of everything. She drifted off, but was jolted rudely out of her daydream as the door burst open, and a gorgeously-dressed redhead swept dramatically into the room.

Joanne followed, protesting. 'I told you, Miss Reynolds, he's not in right now, and he has a visitor.'

'A visitor? Who?' The voice was pure

Deep South, resonant and forceful. Its owner was tall and tiny-waisted, and her flamboyant, jade-green dress made the most of her voluptuous figure.

'Who are you?' she demanded.

Holly, acutely conscious of her dishevelled stickiness, wished she'd spent time in the Ladies' Room, freshening up.

'I'm Holly Peters, from San Maria in Florida. Jade Bay Charters. I'm here to see Jedd about . . . '

'Oh, sure, he tol' me 'bout you.' The tone was disparagingly dismissive. 'It's all right, Joanne. I'll entertain Miss Peters.'

'I don't think . . . ' Joanne began.

'I'm sure you've got work to do.' The redhead glowered at Joanne, who shrugged her shoulders and left them to it. 'I'm Noreen Reynolds.' She held out a hand to touch Holly's briefly. 'You waitin' for somethin'?'

'Jedd. He's coming back. We're going for lunch — after his meeting.'

Noreen raised an eyebrow.

'I don't think so. He's lunching with me today — at The Hyatt Regency. You must have made a mistake.' She flashed her ringed hands at Holly, pointing to a large emerald on her fourth finger. 'Jedd's a very dear, old friend, and today, we're celebrating our engagement. I think you'd be a little intrusive, don't you?' She sat down, picked up a magazine, crossed her shapely legs and smiled sweetly at Holly. She wore a confident, very sure-of-herself smile!

It choked Holly. A pain scalpelled into her, and finally she had to admit the truth to herself. She was deeply in love with Jedd Rivers! That's why she'd come all this way to see him in Atlanta — not really for advice on Jade Bay. The problems there were insignificant compared with the huge one of a love unreturned. A primitive urge to tear out handfuls of Noreen's silky, red hair was so strong it frightened Holly. The humiliation was too much to bear. It was imperative to get away. At once!

'I must have made a mistake!' she

said, as calmly as she could. 'Would you tell Mr Rivers I've gone back to San Maria? I'll be in touch.'

'Sure will.' Noreen idly flicked the pages, and didn't look up until Holly had left the room.

The drive back was busy, but Holly was a good driver, and set herself on automatic while she tried to cope with the pain of her love for Jedd. What an idiot she'd been, rushing off to Atlanta! Of course, a man as attractive and powerful as Jedd would have a string of girlfriends. He and Noreen were well suited. He'd never led Holly to believe he was unattached. True, he'd kissed her, and she felt he was attracted to her, but that was no reason for her to believe he could be in love with her. No wonder she hadn't missed Dave, and wasn't the slightest bit interested in Andy — it was Jedd she'd wanted all the time. Well, too bad — he was spoken for.

She tried to rationalise her confused thoughts, but her heart refused to be silenced. How long, before the pain would ease? Perhaps the answer would be to leave San Maria, where everything reminded her of Jedd.

She drove out of Georgia, on through Alabama, and back down to the Florida Coast. When she let herself into her apartment, the telephone was ringing. Wearily, she picked it up, registering the howling sound of the wind shaking the windows. She had hardly noticed the weather when she was driving, her mind too occupied with thoughts of Jedd.

'Holly!' The voice was whiplash angry. 'What the blazes do you think you're playing at? Why'd you run out like that?'

'Jedd! I . . . '

'I told you to wait. I'd arranged for you to meet Aunt Cass. What was the point of driving all the way up here, and then going straight back again? It's that family trait — pure stubbornness. Your grandfather was just the same.'

'How do you know?' Holly flared.

'You never met him, and don't tell me what to do . . . '

'Look — it's not safe there.' Jedd adopted a calmer tone.

'Safe! Don't be silly. It's only the Environmental Lobby who . . . '

'Haven't you heard the radio at all? Seen the television news? The last thing the authorities are worrying about at the moment is your reef wreck. Hurricane Pat has veered and its course is straight for the Northern Gulf coast. Pack your things. Get out now!'

8

There was a thunderous knocking and bell chiming at her apartment door, and she could hear a voice shouting. She dropped the phone, and ran to open the door. Andy was leaning against the bell.

'For heaven's sake, where've you been? There's all hell let loose at Jade Bay. Some pollution problem with the reef, and you took all the schedules with you. Plus the hurricane warnings are out. We've been working all day securing the boats. Crystal and Brett are still there. If Hurricane Pat hits this part of the coast, you can say goodbye to Jade Bay Charters.'

'Oh, Andy! I'm so sorry. I went to Atlanta — to see Jedd. I was worried . . . '

'You were worried! Couldn't you at least have left a message? Or mebbe even talked to us?'

'I should've done. No excuses.' Contrition, annoyance at her lack of thought overwhelmed her. She grabbed her jacket. 'How long have we got?'

'Oh, hours yet, and it may change course, but we can't take risks. You'll need to pack all your documents. But if there is a final alert, we just leap into the nearest vehicle and go like fury. Come on. My car's outside.'

'Shouldn't I pack a few things here first?'

'No time. You can come back. We'll leave a time margin.'

Holly looked out beyond the deck and, for the first time, recognised the menace approaching. Grey walls of water were slowly building up. The wind was still no more than ordinary storm force, but it was enough to bend the fronded palm trees at the edge of the beach.

'It's so flat here. One big wave surge, and Silver Shores would be the first place to disappear!'

'Andy, don't scare me! Come on, let's go.'

'A fine time to take off for Atlanta.' Andy was still grumbling when they reached Jade Bay Charters.

Holly apologised profusely to the staff, who'd been beavering away all day, transferring equipment, via pick-up trucks, to the higher lying towns of Granville and Valparaiso. Guilt-stricken by their weariness, she worked as hard as she could to complete the security process. They stayed tuned to the radio, and received hourly bulletins. Traffic was already streaming north, although the hurricane was still out in the Gulf.

Brett announced that he had little faith in the State's accurate forecasting, and it was time they went. They'd done as much as they could.

'I must go back to Silver Shores to get some things.' Holly pushed her hair out of her eyes. The air had turned sultry and they were all dripping with sweat.

'You'd better come with us,' Crystal said. 'My family's in Granville — well away inland.'

'I couldn't impose . . . '

'Oh, for goodness' sake, don't be so
— so — English!' Crystal snapped. 'It's
that or a motel. Take your pick.'

Holly would actually have preferred a
motel, but felt Crystal, prickly as she
was, would be even further offended.
'Thank you,' she said meekly. 'I'll have
to go home first though.'

'Please yourself. Don't be too long
though. The next twenty-four hours
will be crucial. Here's the address.
Head for Highway 89, keep going,
and Granville's about fifty miles on.'

'Just blast your way through the
traffic,' Brett added. 'You coming, too,
Andy?'

'Maybe later. I'll just see to my folks
first. Make sure they're OK. Will you be
all right, Holly?'

'Certainly will.' She sounded much
calmer than she felt, and envied the
matter-of-fact attitudes of the others.
'Aren't you worried?' she couldn't help
asking.

'Seen it all before. You get kinda

fatalistic about it after a while. It's never hit San Maria, so you think it never will. Still, we have to act as though it's going to.' Crystal shrugged into her coat, and looked round the barren room. 'Hope to see you again soon, Jade Bay. Let's go!'

Holly had a case full of documents, and the rest of the stuff had been loaded on the pick-up. It took her an hour to get back to Silver Shores, the outgoing traffic was so dense.

At one point, she wondered whether she should carry on with the main stream going north, but Grandad's letter and documents were at the apartment, and she needed personal things. The latest bulletin was more reassuring — Pat was moving North East, and might only just clip the edge of the Emerald Coast.

It was nearly three o'clock when she turned into the parking lot of the apartment building. It was very dark, and the block seemed deserted. No-one in their right minds would stay so close to the water in the circumstances!

It took a few moments to pack what she wanted. She'd hardly slept the previous night, and was deathly tired and sticky. The wind had dropped away, and there was a strange calm. Surely there'd be time to snatch a quick shower to wake herself up for the drive north?

The phone was still dangling off the hook. She'd forgotten about it, and replaced it now. At least there had been too much activity to give a thought to Jedd. The shower water was bliss. She turned the dial to needle jet, and let it sting and stab her weariness away. Gasping, she switched it off, and turned to step out of the cabinet.

Her scream sounded piercingly shrill in the silent flat. She cowered back in panic, hands across her, as a tall shadow filled the glass screen.

'Holly? Holly? Are you in there?'

Her knees nearly collapsed, as wild relief replaced hysterical fear. 'Jedd!'

'Here.' He slid open the door a

fraction and passed her a towel. 'Hurry, Holly. Why you have to choose now to take a shower I'll never know.'

'I was sticky, and very tired.' She wrapped the towel round her and stepped into the bathroom — straight into Jedd's arms.

He held her for a moment, then gave her a gentle push. 'Get dressed.' His voice was husky. 'Have you got what you want to take with you?'

'Yes, but . . . '

'No buts. Just hurry. Where were you heading?'

'Crystal's family — in Granville.'

'Put your clothes on while I phone her.'

'Why?'

'Because you're coming with me.'

'But Jedd, Noreen . . . '

'Stop butting, I said. And I haven't brought Noreen with me. Now move!'

He took her arm and led her from the darkened building, explaining as they went that he'd flown from Atlanta in a company jet to the local air force base. The car was a borrowed one. He was taking her to his family house near White River State Park, close to the Alabama state line.

Holly heard his calm, reassuring voice, as if in a dream. She was so tired, it was wonderful to have Jedd in charge. She leaned her head against the cushioned head rest, and went to sleep.

She woke to a white, wet, dawn light and the sound of scrunching gravel. She yawned and blinked. As memory returned, a warm glow of happiness filled her being. It wasn't a dream — Jedd was by her side.

'Here we are. Swan Plantation House, our original ancestral home. My grandfather was born and raised here. When we moved to Atlanta, my parents couldn't part with it. We use it as a holiday place. It's closed up now, but it'll do us until the hurricane's blown over.'

'What's the news?'

'Getting closer, but veering off to the east a bit. With a bit of luck, San Maria might get away with it.'

Holly got out of the car and gasped at the imposing square, white building in front of her. 'Jedd, it's huge!' She could scarcely believe her eyes.

'It's pretty fine, isn't it? Pre-civil war, like so many houses in this part of the south. You should see Aunt Cass's place. She was pretty mad you ran out on us. She was counting on meeting you yesterday.'

'I shouldn't have gone to Atlanta in the first place,' Holly murmured, a flush on her cheeks.

'Why did you come down, Jedd?'

'Let's get inside, shall we?' he suggested. 'No point in getting any wetter than we have to.'

The rain was sheeting down, but Jedd had parked so near the imposing, porticoed entrance that, within seconds, they were inside.

'Wow!' Holly looked at the vast entrance hall, and wide, central staircase sweeping up both sides to a galleried upper floor. 'Isn't there anybody else here?'

Jedd's blue eyes were lazy. He wore casual jeans and sweatshirt and looked much more like the Jedd she'd first met on Sea Jade I.

'There's a couple who caretake for us, but they're not here right now. If Jeannie had been here, she'd have had a real southern breakfast ready for us. As it is, you'll have to make do with my catering.'

'But what about Noreen, your fiancée?'

Jedd took her hand. 'Come on — to the kitchen. You can help. You can also leave Noreen to me.'

In the vast, well-modernised kitchen, Jedd cooked scrambled eggs, bacon and grits, a mushy sort of semolina he'd flavoured with cheese. The aroma of fresh coffee filled the room, and Holly realised she was hungry and thirsty. She attacked her breakfast with relish.

'You don't seem to have lost your appetite,' he remarked as she cleared her plate in record time.

'Sorry. Was I greedy? You shouldn't

be such a good cook. That was great.'

Jedd poured more coffee and smiled. 'Glad you enjoyed it. But now, you should finish your sleep out. Jeannie keeps the beds well aired.'

'What about you?'

'I've brought some work to do. There's a Fax machine here so, unless the lines are down, I'll be able to get quite a bit done.'

There was a pause, then Holly felt she had to ask him.

'Jedd, tell me — why did you come?'

'I was worried about you. When the phone call was broken off, I couldn't get through again, and there was something wrong with the Jade Bay Charter line. Then the hurricane . . . and . . . ' The deep, sapphire eyes held hers. 'We have lots of unfinished business, you and I, Holly. That's why I was so angry when you ran away.'

'Miss Reynolds — Noreen — told me you were engaged.'

'Was that why you ran off? Trust Noreen!' His voice was grim.

'But is she your fiancée?'

'Noreen Reynolds is . . . ' The phone shrilled urgently, and with an impatient gesture, Jedd went to answer it. He listened for a while, nodding, then said, 'Hold on.'

He covered the mouthpiece with his hand, while he spoke to Holly. 'It's the office in Atlanta. This'll take quite a while. You go up — choose a bedroom. There're plenty up there. No, I'll clear away. You get some sleep.' He turned back to the phone.

With a tired shrug, Holly picked up her bag and went slowly up the stately staircase. The en-suite bathroom was a modern dream, but the bedroom itself was pure colonial, with a high, four-poster bed and lace quilt. Its snowy sheets looked so inviting, she quickly undressed, tumbled in among the pillows and went straight to sleep.

A howling wind woke her some hours later. For a few seconds, in the unfamiliar historical setting, she couldn't recall where she was, or how she'd got there. When she'd found her bearings again, she went to the window and looked out. Jedd's borrowed car was still by the porch.

The grounds stretched away to a distant lake, and wind and rain swayed the mossed, Spanish oaks around the house. To Holly, the place was just like a movie set, a scene from 'Gone With The Wind.'

She clutched a towelling robe to her, as Jedd came in at that moment.

'Sorry. I did knock,' he said mildly. 'Do you want some tea?'

'Tea?'

'We keep it specially for Cass. She's a tea freak — hates coffee. In the library in five minutes.'

When Holly went downstairs, there was a log fire burning in the white-panelled library, with a tea tray on a low table by a sofa. Jedd was reading, but when Holly came in, he put down the book, took her in his arms and kissed her full on the mouth. She struggled briefly — he was engaged to someone else! But the sweet tide swept through her again, obliterating guilt and reason. Her lips clung to his, her body moulded to his. Outside, the wind howled and the rain beat on the shingled roof with increased ferocity. Holly tried to pull away, but Jedd held her more strongly to him.

'No,' he said hoarsely, kissing her again.

'But, Noreen.'

He gave her a little shake. 'Noreen is not my fiancée. Never was — never will be.' His mouth sought hers again and at last she felt free to respond willingly.

After a time, they drew apart. Jedd moved her to the sofa and sat beside her.

'Tea, I think, before it's a total write-off. I have to talk to you, Holly, so stop looking at me like that. Maybe I'd better sit over here.' He handed her a cup and saucer and moved to the corner of the sofa.

'But why did Noreen say . . . ?'

Jedd gestured impatiently. 'It's too

long a story for now but, if you must know — briefly, Noreen is a very old friend — and a dear one. Our families are tied up together in business. She wants to be an actress. Well, she fell for some producer guy, who wouldn't bite. She's a volatile girl, and once she's got a hold on something, she won't give up. As a final try, she pretended she was engaged to me, to make him jealous, I guess, let him see what he was missing! That's all. She'd no call to tell you we were engaged, but that's Noreen — never could resist playing her big part to the full!'

'Did it work?'

'How should I know? Let's forget Noreen, shall we? She's plagued me enough this last month, one way and another. It's your grandfather's will I want to talk about. I told you I've seen Cassie. What she had to say convinced me you should act quickly. I think you should see your solicitor right away — as soon as the hurricane alert's over.'

'But I've barely done more than a

couple of months.'

'I know that, but you've proved you can run Jade Bay.'

'The terms are . . . '

'Holly,' Jedd broke in, 'I think it may be dangerous for you to carry on.' His voice held a very serious note and Holly's eyes widened. 'What?'

'Don't you see? All the things going wrong,' he persisted. 'If you stay another month, goodness' knows what else might happen to you.'

'No-one could have engineered the hurricane,' she protested.

'Of course not. I mean all the other mishaps. And Fred told Cassie more than she let on. I know Homer Rechts, your solicitor. I'll come with you, as soon as we're back in San Maria.'

'What did your aunt tell you?'

'Let's just wait until we've seen Homer. There'll be no-one there now, and it'll take a day or two for things to get back to normal, providing the hurricane doesn't score a direct hit on San Maria. If it does, Jade Bay won't be viable for weeks anyway!'

'When will we know?'

Jedd glanced toward an antique grandfather clock. 'Later tonight. We'll catch the news. Now, let's get back to where we were.' Solemnly, he handed her a plate of English muffins.

Later, they switched on the television set and, to their relief, Pat had given San Maria a miss, whirling eastwards. Holly watched Jedd's profile as he reached forward to switch off the set.

'I'm sorry for those farther east, but pleased for us.' She felt a sense of anti-climax.

Jedd threw more logs on to the flickering fire. 'It's always like this. Big buildup of tension, then wham! The elastic snaps.'

'Shouldn't you let the fire die down? We can go back now.' Holly's spirits were sinking lower by the minute. She certainly hadn't wanted Hurricane Pat to hit Jade Bay but, guiltily, she was enjoying the adventure with Jedd.

'Go back?' he repeated. 'Not tonight

we can't. It's late, and I need a night's sleep. We haven't all been slumbering the day away.'

Holly flushed. 'I'm sorry. Of course, you must be worn out. You didn't get any sleep last night, but . . . isn't it . . . won't it . . . ?' She floundered, and Jedd's mouth curved into a broad grin.

'Are you trying to tell me that you don't think it's proper for us to spend the night together — alone?' He gave the words dramatic emphasis.

'Don't laugh at me. I didn't mean . . . ' Her cheeks were still warm.

He moved closer to her, putting his arm about her shoulders. 'And I thought you were a woman of the Nineties. That's what you told me, back in San Maria.'

Their faces were almost touching. Holly couldn't take her eyes away from his mouth. Softly, he brought it down on hers, but the touch was light, and he held himself in check.

'Holly Peters, I did not bring you here with evil intent. I brought you here because it was safer than sitting on the beach at Silver Shores waiting for a possible strike from Hurricane Pat. If I'd wanted to force myself on you, I'd have had plenty of opportunity, without waiting for the conventional — er — bedtime!'

He punctuated his speech with butterfly touches, causing every vertebrae on Holly's spine to quiver and shift. He moved away. 'When will you learn to trust me, Holly?'

She didn't answer. In this case, it wasn't Jedd she mistrusted — it was herself! Every minute, she was falling more and more in love with the attractive and honourable American.

★   ★   ★

Homer Rechts looked at Holly curiously. A remarkably pretty girl, he thought, and there was no mistaking her resemblance to Fred Peters. He thought a while, before answering her question.

'Yes, I knew your grandfather quite well. An unusual man, I'd say.' He nodded to Jedd. 'Your Aunt Cassie recommended us to Mr Peters. I had a phone call from her this morning, curiously enough.'

'Not really. I spoke to her myself last night from Swan Plantation House. I took Holly up there to be safe.'

'Wise precaution, although we were fortunate this time.'

Holly fidgeted impatiently. There'd been a good deal of polite, verbal fencing. She was glad Jedd was with her. Homer Rechts gave the impression that, had she been on her own, he wouldn't have taken her request to curtail her apprentice spell at Jade Bay at all seriously. He'd hummed and hawed, and consulted his partner in the next office, until Jedd himself had lost patience.

'Aw, come on, Homer. You know it's OK. Holly's proved she can run the company. There aren't any problems.'

'I did hear whispers . . . '

'Malicious rumours.' Jedd stood up angrily, and Holly had asked Homer Rechts about her grandfather mainly to diffuse the tension. The ploy had worked.

The lawyer came to a decision. 'Very well. Miss Rivers has a stake in Jade Bay anyway, which puts a slightly different complexion on things. In the circumstances, I don't see what harm it could do to release the documents. I'll have to inform Spencer and Chapman, in London, naturally.'

'That's not a problem.' Holly tried to control her breathing, and entirely unconsciously, clutched Jedd's hand as Mr Rechts pulled out a large, manilla envelope from his desk drawer. He seemed reluctant to part with it, turning it over and over in his fingers.

'Do you know what's in it?' Jedd asked, keeping a firm grip on Holly's hand.

'I have an idea. Because Miss Rivers recommended us, Mr Peters was able to be fairly frank with us.' He tapped the envelope. 'This could be dynamite. Dangerous dynamite, should anyone else get hold of it! I suggest you guard it very carefully, Miss Peters.'

She took it from him. 'Of course I will — and, thank you.'

'Aren't you going to open it here?'

'Oh, no. I need to be — somewhere private.'

He nodded agreement. 'I wish you every success with your grandfather's final testament. Good-day, Miss Peters.'

9

When they left the lawyer's office, Jedd held her hand tightly as they made their way back to the car. 'I'll run you back to Silver Shores,' he offered.

'I ought to check at Jade Bay first,' she reminded him but, as usual, he was one step ahead of her.

'I've already done that. I phoned Crystal. They'll be working there this morning, taking the equipment back. There's no call for you to rush over straight away. It'll be a while before the tourists come back. Even a sniff of a hurricane is bad for business.'

Holly smiled secretly, unable to help herself. At least the hurricane had brought Jedd back, she thought . . .

Back at Silver Shores, there were one or two cars in the parking lot. Normality was returning, but not, it was soon clear, to Holly's life.

'Oh, no!' She gasped as she opened the door of her apartment. 'Not again.'

Jedd followed closely and exclaimed at the sight of the dishevelled sitting room.

'Looks like the hurricane hit here at least.'

Holly pulled the envelope from her bag. 'Do you think this is what he — or she — was after?'

'Very likely. The hurricane warning was perfect cover. Everyone evacuated. Looks like a thorough search this time.'

'They might have tidied up a bit.' Holly pushed aside a pile of up-ended books, and sat on the sofa. 'Quite a risk for whoever it was, with Hurricane Pat threatening!'

'Obviously they felt that what they were looking for was worth it.'

'Let's see if they were right.' Holly turned the envelope over. 'Jedd, will you stay while I read this?'

'Of course — if you want me to.'

'I think I do.'

'You trust me?'

'I have to.'

Slowly, Holly slit the seal and pulled out the contents. There was a letter in Fred's hand, shorter this time, and a wad of documents banded together. She put those on one side.

After a few minutes, she lifted her eyes and stared at Jedd. 'He mentions you,' she whispered, and passed him the letter.

He scanned the page rapidly, dark eyes widening. 'So, Cass was right — it is a treasure trove!'

'It must be fantasy — a Spanish galleon, sunk in the seventeenth century, out in the Gulf of Mexico.'

'No, it's not fantasy,' Jedd said, a tremor or excitement in his voice. 'There were lots of ships around at that time. Spain was enormously wealthy from the riches of her South American colonies. There was piracy, too. Jean Lafitte, one of the most notorious pirates, had headquarters around here. Reputedly, there's still treasure buried under the dunes. And the Donna

Isabella, the galleon Fred writes of, was legendary. Lots have tried, but no-one's succeeded in locating it. It looks as though this friend — or partner — your grandfather met, finally cracked it.' His eyes shone with wild excitement, and he picked up the banded documents. 'May I?'

Holly nodded, still trying to take it in, re-reading the letter. It was factual and impersonal — Fred had expended his emotional store on the first one.

My dear girl, she read, *so you've come this far. Well done. Now you know about Jade Bay — and you'll have met Jedd Rivers. Cassie told me about him. He's coming to Jade Bay while I'm out on my trip.*

So, Fred had written his will before his last expedition. She skipped to the last paragraph.

So Juan Santos finally gave me all the information he'd gathered about Isabella over the decades, just before he died. I'd hoped we'd be together, Holly, but it's not to be. Take care how you do it. You'll need help — maybe Cassie's nephew? Brett? Crystal? You must judge whether you can trust them. Lust for gold can quickly turn a character! Juan Santos was a bitter recluse, and maybe it's affected me, too. All I seem to think about is that lost ship, Donna Isabella, on the sea bed somewhere, with a fortune, fabulous beyond man's dreams. And it's all for you, Granddaughter. Visit Cass Rivers some time. You'll owe her some of it. I loved her once. Not as I loved Emily, but . . . The writing tailed off, as though he was tired, or it was too much of a burden. She reached the final sentence.

. . . relevant documents. Take care, dearest Holly. Good luck, and be happy.

She swallowed down the familiar stone of grief, and laid the letter on her lap. Jedd was absorbed in the documents, studying them with a frown of intense concentration. He looked up suddenly and Holly was startled by his expression.

'Jedd?' His look had almost had a glitter of fanaticism in it, but it was gone so quickly, she dismissed it as imagination. He was clearly excited.

'Everything's here! Location, references, authenticated copies of documents of the period. The list of bullion's here. Imagine all the jewellery and the personal effects of the travellers. Think of the history there, too!'

'But someone else knows about it.' Holly gestured to the disarray. 'There's someone trying to drive me away from Jade Bay. Even that telephone call about environmental problems on the reef. While I was in Atlanta, he telephoned again. Crystal put him off. She seemed to think it was a hoax.'

Jedd nodded but leaned forward purposefully, bundling the documents together.

'Anyway, whoever it is doesn't know you've got these.'

'True. But what do I do now?' Holly was still reeling from the shock.

Jedd gave her a curious look. 'That's

up to you.' He held up the bundle of papers. 'Isn't this what you came to Florida for?'

'I didn't know it would entail a massive undertaking like this. It would cost the earth, wouldn't it? How Fred thought he'd get the money . . . '

'From Aunt Cass, I suspect. Of course, to raise the wreck would be out of the question, but to explore it is a possibility. The ocean's been crowded with treasure seekers for centuries — so much so, that since 1967, the state of Florida has placed all wrecks in her waters under the jurisdiction of the Department of State for Preservation.'

'Does that mean I can't go?

'You can certainly take a look. After that, who knows? There's a deal of illegal hunting going on under the guise of diving holidays — just to look at the fish!'

'Jedd?' Holly was tentative, and he looked at her quizzically. 'Do you think you could . . . ?'

'Just try keeping me away.' He

laughed. 'Aunt Cass would never speak to me again if I missed a chance like this. We'll have to have Brett and Crystal along, too. Andy can keep Jade Bay Charters afloat. We shouldn't be gone long. It's not more than a hundred miles from here, assuming the weather settles.'

'I'd rather take Andy and leave Crystal and Brett here,' Holly said, hesitantly.

'No. We'll need a third diver, and someone to help out on the boat, too.'

'Third diver? Crystal?'

'No. I've done a fair bit. Same level as you.'

She stared. 'You never told me.'

'You never asked.'

There was a strange tension between them, which held until Holly asked, 'Must Crystal and Brett know everything?'

'My guess is that they already suspect something. With all the promises about making them rich, Fred must have intended taking them along. There's no alternative, Holly.'

She still looked mutinous. Her innate distrust of Crystal was hard to shift, but sure enough, Fred had mentioned them. Jedd was right, she didn't have a choice.

She started to tidy the books. 'Let's go as soon as we can, before whoever's responsible for this gets there first.'

'Give me time to sort things out in Atlanta. You brief the others, and make sure you've got all the right equipment. Then, as soon as the weather's OK, we'll be off. Shall I give you a hand here?'

'No thanks. It looks worse than it is. You must be getting back. And thanks, Jedd.'

'For?'

'Everything. Everything you've done.'

'My pleasure. One more thing — I'll take charge of these.' He waved the documents. 'Not the letter, but the maps and the documents are, as Homer so rightly put it, dynamite. You and your flat are too vulnerable. I'll put them in my bank until we're ready to go.'

'But . . . ' Holly couldn't think of a sensible reason why she wanted to keep Fred's papers herself. 'I can change the locks again.'

'This particular burglar isn't going to be deterred by a new lock. He's already proved that.'

He stuffed the papers in his pocket, then came to her, taking her face in his hands. His touch thrilled through her body, and as his lips touched hers in a farewell kiss, she knew she would always love Jedd Rivers, and that she would gladly give him all the treasure aboard the Donna Isabella, if he found he could love her in return!

After he'd gone, she started to tidy up. The intruder hadn't done any damage, merely left the contents of every drawer, cupboard and shelf on the floor. She took out the vacuum cleaner and was about to tackle the floor when she noticed something glittering under the sofa. She bent to pick it up, and found it was a dangly, gold and coral earring. She recognised it immediately as one of a favourite pair of Crystal's. Crystal must have worn it the night they all came back to Silver Shores, after dinner at The Back Porch.

Then she froze. Crystal had been wearing a bright, red dress that evening! The orange coral lay in Holly's palm. Crystal would never have worn the two colours together. She was a wildly, flamboyant dresser, but her taste was good. That dress and these earrings would have shrieked disharmony.

Holly closed her eyes, desperately trying to remember that evening. It was too hazy. Maybe the dress wasn't bright red after all. Gold sandals came into the picture, but not the earrings. She tried hard to visualise them under Crystal's bright curls — they must have been there. If not, it could mean only one thing! Crystal had been here on another occasion, when Holly herself was not in residence.

The night of the hurricane warning,

Crystal had gone to Granville — but had she gone straight there? Had she known Jedd was going to turn up, to take Holly away? But hadn't Crystal herself offered her sanctuary at Granville?

Holly put the earring in a box, then switched on the cleaner. Crystal just had to have worn them that night, otherwise it would mean that not only was Crystal suspect, and probably Brett, but Jedd as well. That was unthinkable! But why had Jedd been so keen to take the documents away? Could Cassie Rivers be in this, too?

As Holly whirred the cleaner round the apartment, she remembered the glimpse of the first intruder, and her conviction that it was female. She switched off the machine. It was very quiet. Shafts of sunlight were creeping back after the storms. She concentrated her thoughts on her grandfather, trying to fathom out an answer, holding his letter to her heart. Nothing — no sense of guidance! She sighed, iritated by her own superstitious behaviour. She knew what he'd have said anyway — 'Trust your own judgement, girl. Make your mind up, and stick with it.' There really was no choice.

* * *

Sea Jade II rocked gently on aquamarine water. After the threatened devastation of Hurricane Pat, the weather decided on a tranquil Indian Summer, which was perfect for Expedition Isabella. Holly and Brett had modified and equipped Sea Jade II for deep-sea diving, and a week after Homer Rechts had released the second part of Fred Peter's will, the boat was anchored according to the precise instructions of Juan Santos' map, about fifty miles out from the West Coast.

A couple of exploratory dives the previous day had yielded nothing. Today, Jedd and Brett proposed to explore the deeper water on the other side of the reef where Juan Santos had believed Donna Isabella had foundered.

Holly was gathering her equipment,

ready to go down later. She checked the time. The two men had been gone nearly an hour. Their fifteen-litre air tanks had sufficient air for the hour, and they had a small, emergency tank between them. Nevertheless, the arrangement was that they should surface on the hour. She circled the deck, but there was no sign of the divers in any direction.

Suddenly, she was conscious of a roar in the distance. She saw Crystal point northwards, where, the day before, a large yacht had been anchored. Screaming towards them was a power boat, its prow so high in the water, it appeared to be standing on end.

The spray thrown up obscured the figure at the wheel. Holly glimpsed dark glasses and a black wet-suit, as the boat came on. She saw, rather than heard, Crystal's scream of anger as it came within inches of ramming them, before it veered off to the horizon. The wash rocked Sea Jade, as Crystal stormed down to the lower deck.

'What on earth was all that about?

What a maniac! I thought he was going to hit us. He was like some sort of kamikase pilot. If Jedd or Brett had surfaced just then . . . ' She shuddered. 'Anyway, they should be up now. They're overdue.'

'Look, there's one of them — it's Brett.' A black head bobbed on the surface, to be joined by another. 'Thank goodness — they're both safe.'

The two divers, looking a little like alien, sea monsters, clambered on board, shrugged off their heavy cylinders, and undid their weight belts. Holly knew they'd found it, even before Jedd had pulled off his mask. She could sense it.

'It's there! The other side of the reef, caught on a ledge about sixty feet down.' Brett's voice was awed. 'I can't believe it. Just like that.' He took off his dry-suit. 'The old men were right. And we took them for crazy fools!'

'What's it like? Can you see much? I'm going down now.' Excitement spilled out of Holly.

'Hold on. You can't go down on your own. We'll rest, then go with you. There's a lot of silt, but the shape's unmistakeable. It's about eighty feet long, thirty-five-foot beam, I'd say. We'll take the hand blowers down to clear the sand and shells — see if there's anything around to prove it's Donna Isabella.'

'But it must be.' Crystal caught the excitement, her anger forgotten.

'It probably is, but hey, what was all that commotion just before we surfaced?' Jedd took off his fluorescent jacket.

'Some idiot in a power boat — from the yacht we saw anchored yesterday.'

Jedd frowned. 'There's no other registered vessel in this area. I checked last night with the Coastal Station.'

'Lots of illegal ships out here.' Brett was laconic. 'Drug running — illegal immigrants from Mexico — could be anything.'

'Why advertise yourself with a high-speed power exhibition then?'

'Come on, Jedd, forget it,' Holly begged. 'I can't wait to get down there.'

Holly felt close to the realisation of her goal — the thing that had excited and obsessed her grandfather during the last months of his life. If she could see the wreck, just touch it, it would somehow justify that obsession. Beyond that, she had no plan. Excitement coursed through her being. She'd cast off doubts and suspicions and accepted Crystal's and Brett's presence on the expedition without contemplating any treachery on their part. She'd made her decision and would abide by it.

They had coffee and sandwiches on the sunlit deck. No-one spoke much. It was an awesome time, as they imagined the ship beneath them, the drowned bodies, long reduced to bone and dust.

'Such a relatively small object in a vast expanse of ocean, and it's right here.' Jedd voiced the wonderment they all felt. 'Years of work by Juan Santos, but he's dead, so he'll never know . . . '

'What about his family? Surely they

have a right to know.' Holly was beginning to realise some of the implications of the discovery.

'He hated them,' Crystal told her. 'He didn't tell us much, but he did say that he'd quarrelled with them years ago. He was very rich, had made a fortune when he was young, and was spending every penny on this search for the Donna Isabella, though we didn't know that at the time. He was so paranoid and secretive — your grandfather was his only friend.'

Impulsively, Holly jumped up and reached for her dry-suit. 'Please — let's go. It'll be dark soon.'

'Donna Isabella's been down there over three centuries — she won't go away today. Why don't we leave it now? We can go in the morning.' Jedd was stretched out on the deck reading the charts and notes again. He shook his head. 'The work here is amazing. One man's lifetime quest — and we're the beneficiaries. Seems unfair, doesn't it? There's a letter here in Spanish, too. I haven't had time to translate.'

'Jedd!' Holly was jumping with impatience. 'You've had your moment of history. Let me have mine.'

Jedd opened his mouth to protest again, but seeing the despair on her face, he grinned.

'OK, OK. We know where we're going so it won't take long. Ready, Brett?'

'Absolutely!'

The three of them kitted up, checking each other's equipment meticulously. Crystal had already moved Sea Jade over the exact spot where they'd pinpointed the wreck.

One after the other, the three figures rolled easily backwards into the clear water. The finned downwards, keeping together. As they went deeper, the cut-glass surface of the sea disappeared, and they floated in a hazy, blue infinity.

Jedd, slightly ahead, stopped and pointed to a sand-shrouded shape, with rounded hull, masts and spars sticking out at odd angles.

The elation of discovery was almost overwhelming, mingled as it was with sadness for the drowned souls, and for the proud ship humbled in its watery grave. Holly turned to Jedd, who was watching her closely. She could see his eyes clearly behind the mask, and she gave the thumbs-up sign of success.

Jedd held up the blower and started to sweep along the surface near the wreck. Brett was behind. She signalled her intention of going closer to the wreck. Jedd mimed, 'Take care,' then he and Brett concentrated on the shifting sand, hoping to turn up some artefact from the ship itself.

Holly checked her air level. Half a tank — thirty minutes left. She finned along to the prow of the wreck, cautiously keeping away from the actual timbers. It still looked very solid, but she knew that if a rogue current carried her against it, it could unsettle its stability. There was some sort of figurehead angled away to the right. Looking back, she saw Jedd and Brett were out of sight.

She must have moved farther along than she'd intended. Turning to go back, a shoal of colourful fish darted by, and the sand swirled and eddied around her. An air check showed fifteen minutes left — it was time to start back, but there was still no sign of the others. Jedd would be furious — she'd committed the cardinal sin of losing contact. They must be close.

She finned back along the line of the hull. Maybe they'd drifted away, but it was unlikely. In a few minutes, she'd have to start her ascent on her own. She looked over her shoulder, and to her relief, the two figures were behind her. Pointing first to her watch, then upwards, she turned back to start for the surface, taking a last look at the Donna Isabella.

'For you, Grandad,' she said, and joyfully felt that strong sense of his spirit.

But suddenly she realised she was wrong.

At the same moment as she realised it wasn't a comfortable presence, she was grasped from behind, and felt someone tearing at her mask. Lightning reflexes ducked her away, as the dark figures grabbed at her again, this time pinioning her arms tightly to her side, one of them reaching up to the life-giving hose to the air tank.

'Jedd!' she screamed wordlessly — panic and despair choking her more than the threatened cut to her dwindling air supply. Struggling, fighting for her life, her brain screeched out her fatal error of judgement in putting her trust in Jedd Rivers. Descending into whirling blackness, the last thing she saw was a picture of her own body, slumped alongside the doomed Donna Isabella.

10

Warmth, light and voices — one in particular, calling her back . . . she was drifting into an unwanted consciousness. There was a reason. What was it? Jedd! There was something . . .

But it was his voice, anxious, urging. 'Holly, for goodness' sake! Come on.'

She opened her eyes, and saw deep-blue ones above her, darkened almost to black with concern. She tried to sit up, but was gently pushed down. Memory flooded back. He'd tried to drown her! She struggled against the restraining hands.

'No! You tried to take my mask off . . . '

'Holly! Of course I didn't. How could you think such a thing?'

'Who then?'

'Don't talk now. You're still in shock.' Crystal's face, next to Jedd's, was worried and angry. 'Thank goodness you're all right, Holly. For a moment, we thought . . . It was awful. When I saw Jedd and Brett carry you up . . . I could kill them!'

'Jedd? Brett?' Holly was tired, still confused from the almost dangerously rapid ascent from the wreck site.

'No — those awful people. As soon as you'd gone down, a dinghy appeared with two divers. I couldn't warn you — I was frantic.'

'Not now, Crystal. Let her rest.'

Lying in her bunk, Holly hoped it was Crystal who'd removed her dry-suit and wrapped her in a blanket. Her thick hair tumbled round her naked shoulders and Jedd pulled the coverlet up to her throat.

He sat on the edge of the bunk, and took the mug Crystal was holding.

'OK, I'll give her this. You and Brett'd better keep a sharp look-out on deck.'

'Sure thing.' Crystal still looked worried and gave Holly a shaky smile.

'I'm so glad you made it — really.'

Holly smiled back. These people couldn't possibly have tried to kill her and leave her down there with Donna Isabella. Jedd raised her head gently and propped a pillow behind it.

'Hot soup.'

'I'm not an invalid,' Holly protested. Then she was aware of a changed rhythm. 'We're moving — and fast. Why? You must tell me what happened, Jedd.'

'We're getting out of here as fast as possible — to the nearest port, and then to the Coast Guard and police.'

'But — Donna Isabella?'

'Will stay as she is for a while. I'm not risking your life again — not to mention ours. Seeing you in the hands of those — creatures, was the worst moment of my life. We only arrived just in time to chase them off. I should be furious with you for drifting away as you did, but I'm just relieved you're safe.'

'I thought it was you.' Holly was

shame-faced. 'I never thought of anyone else being down there.'

For answer, Jedd put down the soup, leaned across and kissed her long and deeply. He lifted his head, and his hands stroked her cheeks and touched her lips where his had been. 'You've never absolutely trusted me, have you?'

'Yes — no — it was difficult. Crystal was so angry at first, and that break-in, it was a woman, I know it. And I found Crystal's earring on the floor after the second break-in. I don't know what to think.'

'I think you should have said so before and tackled Crystal outright. There has to be an explanation,' Jedd said. 'OK, Crystal was angry but she's no crook.'

'But who else is there, Jedd? Somebody out there wants me out of the way. Why?'

'Why is obvious. You're the legal owner of that treasure trove down there, you and the State of Florida. Men have been known to kill for much,

much less. That's why we're high-tailing it out of here before they have a second go.'

'The yacht — and the power boat? They were the ones?'

'Yup. And we know who they are, thanks to Crystal.'

'Who?'

A shout from up on deck interrupted them, and Jedd sprang to his feet.

'Stay here.'

She heard him run swiftly up the stairs, then Brett shouted again, and Crystal's voice joined in urgently. The engines churned, and Sea Jade surged forward at full throttle.

'I'm hanged if I'm staying here,' Holly muttered, swinging her legs to the floor. She pulled on jeans and a sweater and went up top.

Crystal was up in the wheel-house, determination in every line of her body, willing on Sea Jade as fast as she could. Brett, on the lower deck, had binoculars trained on a motorised yacht, still far off on their port side.

'What is it?' Holly touched his arm, and he spun round.

'Holly! You shouldn't be here. Go back below.'

'I want to know what's going on. Where's Jedd?'

'Calling up the Coast Guard and Marine Police — we need reinforcements! We're still some miles from port, and that thing's gaining on us.' He lifted his binoculars again as Jedd came up.

'Holly, what . . . ?'

'Don't you start. I'm OK. Are they chasing us?'

'They're not doing a practice run. They mean business.'

'I don't believe it.' Brett passed the glasses to Jedd. 'They're armed — and they're getting closer. Two of them have guns.'

Holly's hand flew to her mouth. When she'd been attacked near Donna Isabella, panic, horror and desolation had overwhelmed her, because she'd thought it was Jedd. Fear hadn't been a consideration but now it was. 'What can we do?'

'Nothing. Just hope and pray that Sea Jade can outrun her — or help arrives in time,' Brett said through gritted teeth.

Sea Jade did her best, but the boat behind them was equipped with a far superior engine and the distance between them lessened by the minute. Soon Holly could make out figures on board, and saw that two of them were indeed carrying lethal-looking weapons. There was something very familiar about some of the figures. A woman with long, black hair stood by the deck rail, binoculars trained on Sea Jade. Holly saw the red, white and green flag of Mexico flying from the mast, and she knew who their pursuers were!

She clutched Jedd's arm. 'I know who they are. The flag — it's Mexican!'

He nodded. 'Crystal's realised, too. That recognition that's been teasing her for days. As soon as she saw the man in the dinghy, she made the connection between Paulo Ramirez and the man who called himself Juan Santos.'

'It's the Ramirez! Jamez and Anna are on the boat.'

'And it was Paulo and his father who attacked you.'

'I can hardly believe it. Why should they . . . ?'

'Because they're Juan Santos' estranged family. They've been trailing you ever since you arrived in Florida. You made it pretty easy for them to tamper with your truck, and practically invited them to burgle you.'

'So, it was Anna on the apartment deck that night! But Sea Jade I — could they have had anything to do with its breakdown?'

'We'll never be able to prove it, but Jamez was a mechanic, and was used to nosing around engines. I think they must have thought you'd be discouraged enough to leave Jade Bay.'

'I can't believe it. How could they?'

'You'll soon be able to ask them yourself,' Jedd said grimly. 'They're almost within hailing distance.'

Jedd put his arms around her, but Holly's eyes were fixed on the menacing figures with the guns. It was all her fault. She'd brought them all into danger, chasing a dream!

Then, as Crystal desperately tried to push Sea Jade beyond her limits, the power-boat abruptly altered course and headed away in the opposite direction. A great cheer went up in the wheelhouse, as a couple of high-speed Coast Guard Cutters could be seen approaching. One of them cleaved off through the water on the other boat's trail, the other slowing down quickly to come alongside Sea Jade.

'Not a moment too soon,' Jedd murmured, his arms still round Holly, whose knees had suddenly buckled beneath her.

* * *

Looking back, it seemed to Holly that she'd lived through a Hollywood movie, but she still wasn't sure of the ending.

The Ramirez group had evaded the authorities, and had probably reached Mexico. The teasing likeness of Paulo and his grandfather, Juan Santos, was confirmed in a document amongst the bundle of maps and papers which Fred had left to Holly. The letter, written in Spanish, testified to the acrimony between Juan and his family. It was addressed to Juan Santos Ramirez, and cursed him roundly for neglecting his family duties.

Juan had not used the hated Ramirez name, and his neglected and dishevelled appearance had concealed the family likeness when he was in San Maria. He'd kept the bitter invective amongst his papers — perhaps to fuel his dislike of his relatives, and his determination that they should never share his treasure. Nevertheless, it couldn't have been too difficult for them to trace him, and get some inkling of what he was up to. He'd been obsessed with wrecks, and in particular,

Donna Isabella, for decades.

With Holly's consent, Jedd turned all the information over to the police, who would pass it on to the State Department to decide the fate of Donna Isabella and her treasure.

Once ashore, Crystal and Brett had decided to cruise Sea Jade leisurely back to San Maria and Jedd was to take Holly to meet Cassie Rivers in Atlanta.

It would be the final piece of the puzzle. The Florida adventure was nearly over. Holly hadn't made any plans. Brett and Crystal would be pleased to buy Jade Bay Charters and Holly would be pleased to sell. It held too many memories, too many ghosts, for her to return. And there was no-one she'd rather sell it to. In conference with Crystal, she'd discovered that the mysterious earring had, in fact, belonged to Crystal but it was a pair which Brett had put in his pocket for her, the previous evening, when they'd been out together.

'Déja vu.' Jedd turned up a gravelled drive, and pulled up before a large colonial-style house. 'This time it's the Rivers' Mansion. Aunt Cassie's home.'

It had the same grace and style as Swan Plantation House, but was larger and more grand. The sun was shining, the house looking welcoming, and a beautiful, silver-haired woman was at the door to meet them. She ran down the steps and into Jedd's arms for a huge hug.

'Aunt Cassie! How well you look. Come and meet Holly.'

She embraced Holly, then held her away at arm's length. 'You have Fred's eyes.' She touched the girl's thick, sunstreaked hair. 'That's exactly the colour his was. Come in, come in. I have tea, of course, and a magnificent Creole supper for later. I hope you'll stay a while, my dear.'

'I — I don't know. I haven't any plans, really,' Holly said vaguely.

'Jedd has told me everything that happened. I'm so glad it's all over. I tried to persuade Fred not to carry on, but . . . ' She gave an expressive shrug, and ushered them into a grand drawing room, looking out on to a formal garden.

'This is lovely!' Holly exclaimed.

'Your grandfather loved this garden. I'm so glad he came back to visit me. We had so much to say.' Cassie looked speculatively at Holly. 'He talked of you all the time. His death was a terrible shock but, well, it brought you here.'

'Cassie.' Jedd gave his aunt a warning frown. 'Didn't you say something about tea?'

'Oh — did I? I'd forgotten in the excitement. I'll get it, but first, I want to show you something.'

She took a framed picture from one of many on a bureau and gave it to Holly. Two smiling, very happy, very young people, a girl and a boy, in sepia, over half a century earlier, gazed into each other's eyes. Holly doubted they were even aware of the camera, so absorbed were they in each other's dreams.

'It's Grandad!' she said in surprise.

'Of course. But I know he was happy with your grandmother, and you mustn't feel upset by this. It was long ago.'

'I'm not, and I'm glad to see this.' Somehow, it had nothing to do with Holly. She'd never known that ardent, young man. 'That boy belongs to you,' she said simply, and the two women smiled at each other.

Tears welled in Cassie's eyes, and she hugged Holly. 'Oh, we're going to get along so well, I just know it. I'm so happy — I can't thank you enough. Fred . . . ' She pressed the picture to her heart.

'Cassie! The tea!' Jedd looked sky-wards.

'All right, dear. I'll be straight back.'

Jedd closed the door behind her, then leaned against it. 'Not just yet, Aunt. Please, take your time!'

'Why? She's lovely,' Holly reproved.

'I know, but I need a little time here. I'd planned something more romantic. But the way Cassie's talking, she'll have us married, with three children, before I've had a chance to ask you.'

The world stopped! Holly's heart paused. 'Married,' had he said?

He came towards her, taking her in his arms.

'Before Cass trips in with the tea tray, I love you, Holly. I love you very much. Will you marry me?' His blue eyes were soft as a summer sea, and Holly could have drowned in them. He must know there was no doubt.

'Oh, Jedd. Yes, yes. I love you — so much. I thought — I thought — you didn't love me.'

'Not love you? Why do you think I stayed in San Maria? Why did I go on that crazy expedition?'

'But you left so abruptly. You were away in Atlanta for so long — and there was Noreen.'

'I stayed away because I knew I was

lost if I went back to San Maria. You had a boyfriend, and I did have problems with Noreen. Crystal says you're not interested in Dave, but I'd've taken him on anyway. Life without you would have no joy for me. We'll marry soon.'

She put her arms around his neck, caressing the dark curls she loved so much, and kissed him with such passionate agreement, that neither noticed Aunt Cass bringing in the tea. Cassie watched them for a moment, then coughed delicately. Their lips parted, but Jedd's arms stayed around Holly, who leaned back into their security, blissfully, contentedly, happy.

'Aunt Cass, Holly and I are going to be married.' Jedd stretched out his arm, and brought his aunt into the loving circle.

'I know. I think I always knew it. As soon as Fred appeared and started talking about his magical granddaughter, I thought — she'll be right for Jedd. You'll be married here, I hope. I know you've no family in England, Holly — and you'll have to stay and see what happens to the treasure — all that gold.'

Holly looked up at Jedd, her brown eyes softly radiant. 'I don't care what happens to it. I renounce all claim. It should never belong to me. I have all the riches I want — right here.'

THE END